"**A Bit Of Rough** is a wonderfully romantic and extremely scorching tale. Ms Baumbach gives readers a memorable story and makes you sigh with pleasure. Her characters are men you can't help but care for. Sweet romance and sinfully, blistering sex. What more could you ask for in a good story? How about one that will stay with your for a long time? "

Lisa Lambrecht ..In The Library Reviews

Other Erotic Tales by Laura Baumbach

Out There in the Night
Details of the Hunt
Roughhousing
Mexican Heat
Walk Through Fire
Enthralled
Sin and Salvation

Coming Soon:

The Lost Temple of Karttikeya
Genetic Snare
Entranced
Monster
Ripples on the Moon

Laura Baumbach

A Bit of Rough

This book is a work of fiction. Names, characters, places, and incidents either are products of the author's imagination or are used fictitiously. Any resemblance to actual events or locales or persons, living or dead, is entirely coincidental.

Published by MLR Press, LLC
3052 Gaines Waterport Rd.
Albion, NY 14411

Cover Art by Deana C. Jamroz
Editing by Sue H.

Printed in the United States of America.

ISBN# 0-9793110-1-2
ISBN# 978-0-9793110-1-7

Second Edition
2007

A Bit of Rough

Chapter One

James sat down on the nearest bar stool, ignoring the way his jeans refused to slip over the worn vinyl. He swung one foot back and forth over the broken floor tiles making a gritty sound; the thick leather soles of his boots peeling a layer of dirt off with each pass.

He ordered a Bud from the barmaid, noting the way her C-cups strained against the thin fabric of her low cut halter-top. It was impressive and the blatant, inviting look she gave him in return offered a guarantee of a better look after closing time if he wanted it. James gave her his best 'thanks, but no thanks' smile and sipped his beer, rotating on the stool to get a better view of the rest of the room.

The Atlantic Bar was a biker dive, complete with pool tables, rock and roll music, and a small time drug deal going down just outside the back exit. Led Zeppelin blared out a number on the jukebox and both pool tables had games going. The majority of the patrons were members of the leather and chrome set. Tattoos, tight jeans and shirtless black vests dominated the dress code for both sexes.

This wasn't his usual kind of haunt, but he'd decided earlier tonight to do something unexpected, exciting, and different. So instead of spending a Friday night at home, James Joseph Justin, architect and former altar boy, was cruising a biker bar for a one-night stand. Anyone with a cup size, even a C-cup like the well-endowed barmaid, need not apply.

At five-foot seven, one hundred forty-two pounds, there was nothing physically intimidating or impressive about James, but he could win over almost any problem with his charm and little boy looks. Dark, unruly curls and a pair of wide, sapphire eyes softened even the most resistant during his normal day-to-day interactions. He doubted that would work here if he tried to attract the attention of the wrong guy.

A burst of catcalls and whistles from the far pool table attracted his attention. A deep, soft rumble of laughter cut through the cheers and the background noise to pique James' interest. The sound sent a buzz of arousal through him, making him shift his hips on the stool to ease the sudden tightening of his jeans.

Another murmur of high spirits erupted from the group of men clustered around the end of the table, and James' curious eyes found the source of the low, pleasant voice. Standing between two T-shirted, leather vested, ponytailed bikers was a tall, broad-shouldered, sandy-haired man dressed in denim and cowboy boots. Even from his seat at the bar, James could see the jeans, denim jacket and faded, blue shirt all matched the pale blue of the big man's eyes. James' jeans got a little bit tighter.

The cowboy chalked the end of his cue and moved into place at the end of the table, leaning down to take his shot. Sinking the five-ball in the middle pocket, the man smiled, and glanced up from his conquest, laser blue eyes locking unerringly on James' hungry, unprepared stare. He took his time standing back up, holding James in his sights the entire time, his expression unreadable.

Unable to break away from the mesmerizing stare, James blushed, squirming a little on his stool. Eyes still locked with the stranger's, James watched as the man snagged his beer off the edge of the table and took a drink, arching his neck and swallowing in long, drawn out gulps that made his throat move in an all too-seductive fashion for James' rising libido. After lowering the bottle, the stranger smiled at him, breaking the stare.

James gulped down half his beer and got up to move closer. Taking up a spot by a rough wooden post, he leaned against the support and took another sip of his beer, playing the part of just another interested spectator in the room.

The cowboy rounded the table, studying the lie of the balls, intent on his next move. Picking a tight angle from James' side of the table, the large man bent over to line up his shot, his hip making contact with James as he suddenly pulled back for the shot. James shifted to one side, startled by the unexpected touch. The stranger held the shot, straightened up and stepped in close to him, inhaling deeply.

James' breath turned to soft, little pants at the stranger's abrupt nearness. The man smelt of sweat and leather, a faint, pleasant scent that made James harden against the rough fabric of his jeans. The slight, abrasive rub of the front seam was a relief to the portion of his body seeking more immediate attention.

"Sorry."

James stepped back to give the man room and found himself brought up short against the support beam. The stranger stepped closer, trapping James between himself and the post, a position James wouldn't have minded if they hadn't been in a room full of people. Likely, no one was close enough to overhear any conversation that might take place. The big man was free to flirt or threaten, as the mood struck him. James wasn't sure which, if either, would happen, but he was definitely interested in the tall, hard body currently blocking his view of the room.

James looked up from under his lashes to see an amused, self-assured smile on the man's handsome face. He dropped his gaze, feeling self-conscious and nervous. Did the guy know what he'd been thinking? Could he see the lust in his face, read the willingness in his eyes? Was the smile genuine or just a preamble to punching him out? The same pleasant rumble from earlier drew his gaze back up to the tanned and weathered face in front of him.

"Excuse me. Need a little room to make my move." The cowboy swayed his weight from one foot to the other, his thigh grazing James' hip on the forward motion. He slid the pool cue through his hands, drawing James' gaze down to watch as the cowboy's long fingers stroked over the rod.

James glanced at the few poorly placed balls left on the table. "Doesn't look like you've got much of a shot left."

The big man smiled and glanced over his shoulder at the set up. "Seven ball center pocket." His gaze narrowed, appraising James from head to toe, settling on his clean- face. "After I win, how about I buy you a beer?"

"That's impossible."

Cowboy snorted a dry chuckle. "Which? The shot or buying you a drink?"

James swallowed and huffed out a shaky breath. His nervous habit of biting at his lower lip made the man's eyes flicker down to look at his mouth. James released his lip and licked over the abused flesh, his mouth suddenly dry.

"The shot. No way you can sink the seven-ball in the center pocket. You can't get the angle right." James shook his head, regretting the fact the man was going to lose the game and he would lose the opening for a drink with him. "I know about angles. It's part of my job."

"I like a challenge." One blue eye winked at him. "Decide what kind of beer you want."

There was something possessive and demanding in the soft, gravel tones that made James shiver. He covered his reaction by shrugging his shoulders and relaxing onto the uneven surface of the post at his back.

He nodded. "Okay. If you want to." The stranger held his gaze for a moment longer before smiling and stepping away.

"Oh, I want to." His voice was pitched low, rich and filled with a seductive promise. "This'll just take a minute."

The cowboy rejoined his opponent at the pool table, calling out the shot. The announcement was met with a grunt and a pleased grin from the biker. Seconds later the grin dissolved into a look of awe.

Cowboy spiked the cue ball, skipping it over a blockade of even numbered balls. It ricocheted off the far end at the perfect angle to clip the seven-ball, sending it straight into the center pocket. True to his word, it took him less than a minute to run the table and win the game. He collected his money, hung up his cue stick, and acknowledged the friendly slaps and grudging compliments of the spectators around the table, then walked back over towards James. He flashed a quick smile, showing rows of even, white teeth and a cleft in the middle of his chin. With a tilt of his head, he gestured toward the bar.

James hesitated a moment, then walked to the only empty seat at the bar. Before he could claim it, the stranger stepped ahead of him and swung his taller frame onto the vinyl. James found himself wedged between the man's knees on the left and a biker covered with chains and tattoos on his right.

The cowboy sprawled on the narrow stool, spreading his legs to create more space. Jostled on the right by an unyielding shoulder, James had no choice but to shift into the opening.

The man swiveled the stool, drawing his legs under the counter and bringing James along with them. He rested a knee against the firm surface of James' backside. Smiling at the startled look on James' face, he nonchalantly swiveled the stool back and forth, rubbing his thigh over the swell of flesh. James pressed back against the cowboy's leg, telling him the attention wasn't unwelcome. He trembled against the man's thigh.

Leaning in to make sure he could be heard over the pounding Bob Seager tune, Cowboy flagged the bartender and ordered two bottles of Budweiser. He threw a ten-dollar bill on the bar, picked up both long necks with one hand and stood up. Offering a bottle to James, he ducked close until their cheeks brushed, his prickly, five o'clock shadow bristling against James' smooth face.

"Let's get some air."

Without waiting for an answer, Cowboy started in the direction of the back exit, taking a swallow from his bottle every few feet. He was halfway across the floor before he realized James hadn't followed him. The younger man was still standing at the bar, an uncertain look on his face. The cowboy stood where he was, his gaze locked on James' face, waiting patiently for him to make up his mind.

James could feel the weight of the man's eyes on him, his raw intensity and the heat of his hungry gaze. It pulled at him from across the room, drawing him to the man's side.

The man's gaze never wavered, taking on a satisfied glint as James came to his side. He kept his eyes riveted on James' face, speaking only loud enough for James to hear.

"Do I have to drag you out?"

James felt a shiver of excitement shoot through to his groin. He could barely get his answer out of his tightening throat.

"No."

The man gave James an appraising glance that traveled from head to toe and back again. "But you'd like me to, wouldn't you?" The nervous way James licked his lips was answer enough. Cowboy turned for the back exit. James followed this time.

Once they reached the cooler air of the alleyway, James was forced to stop for a moment to refuse an offer to join a three-man group sharing a pipe. By the time he looked around, the taller man was nowhere to be seen in the dark, narrow lane.

A large, dark red pick-up truck was the only thing in the alley besides a dumpster and several old crates. James took a huge gulp of his beer then set it down on a nearby box. Hesitant, he walked towards the depths of the shadows, squinting to make the most of the pale moonlight.

Three-quarters of the way into the alley, James was suddenly yanked into a deep alcove and slammed up against a wall. A hard body pinned him in place, the sharp edges of the brick surface gouging his back through the thin fabric of his T-shirt. The pain barely registered, as a low, sultry voice by his ear demanded his attention.

"That makes twice you've left me hanging. I don't think I like that."

A knee was forced between his legs and Cowboy's weight settled heavily against his aching groin. James looked up into a pair of hungry eyes that glittered in the dim light. Waves of lust rolled off of his captor, washing over him like pounding surf, dragging him along with the dangerous undertow, and making it hard for him to breathe. A noticeable shudder ran down his spine.

"You're shaking, baby. Excitement…." A callused fingertip ran down the length of his neck and back up to stroke over his open, panting mouth. "Or fear? Doesn't really matter to me." Another shudder rippled through James. Cowboy grinned. "I like you trembling against me, because of me, whatever the reason."

The thigh pressing his legs apart rubbed side to side, massaging the growing bulge in his jeans. James groaned and bit down on one corner of his lower lip to hold back a startled yelp when the pressure increased to the point of near pain.

Cowboy narrowed his eyes, his voice taking on a harsher edge. Warm breath ghosted over James' face, and moist lips grazed against his mouth while the man talked, teasing at the lip tucked between his teeth.

"Does that feel good to you, baby? Like that? Like it slow and gentle?" He lessened the pressure and slipped a hand between them, thumbing open the buttons of James' jeans as he talked. Finding nothing under them except heated flesh, he shoved his hand inside and grabbed James' cock, dragging calluses and fingernails lightly over the sensitive organ. James squirmed and made a strangled, animal sound in the back of his throat.

"No, you wouldn't be on this side of town, in this bar, if gentle was what you were looking for. Maybe you want it a little rougher." He shoved his fingers down farther and captured the tight sac beneath. "A little harder." He massaged James, grinning at the increased squirming and guttural whimpers his heavy caress produced. "A little deeper." Kicking James' legs farther apart, he slid two fingers behind the sac, tracing the thin ridge of sensitive flesh that led up to his opening. Without hesitation, he shoved both fingers into James' body, twisting and stroking the hot, slippery walls of muscle within. A guttural gasp rewarded his efforts.

He chuckled low and throaty, nudging James' cheek with his nose, silently commanding him to look up until their eyes met. "You got yourself all ready for me, baby. All nice", the long agile fingers twisted roughly, "and slick", plunged deeper, "and tight." The questing digits pressed up, grazing over a spongy firmness.

As he fought to remain standing, James spasmed and bucked against the intimate contact. He whimpered and began to pant, arching into the touch while at the same time trying to squeeze shut his thighs. He was torn between the desire to have more from this seductive, intense man and the urge to push the dangerous, aggressive suitor off and stumble back into the bar for a fortifying drink. One more swirling stroke deep inside and desire won.

Jerking his head up, James captured the man's mouth with his own. Both hands tangled in the cowboy's hair, forcing their mouths firmly together. His urgency was met and matched. The kiss was hot and dirty and thrilling, each demanding stroke of tongue met with an equally aggressive suck or bite, until oxygen-deprived, racing heartbeats pounded painfully in their heads.

The cowboy broke away, sliding his fingers out of their tight cocoon of muscle and heat. Pulling his hand from James' jeans, he bestowed a rough caress on James' straining cock on the way out.

"Jesus, fuck!" James protested the loss, thrusting his groin into the retreating hand, his body trying to regain the needed touch.

Cowboy rested his forehead against James', panting heavily. Each warm puff of air sent shivers down James' spine as they trailed over his sweaty flesh.

"Hang on, baby. We're just getting started here."

A quick bite to the exposed curve of James' neck turned into a wet trail that slithered up to his ear. The soft skin behind his ear was mouthed and nipped, making him squirm and arch his neck, offering his throat for attention.

His plea was ignored, the busy lips and tongue choosing the delicate morsel of his ear lobe instead. A rhythmic sucking mimicked the earlier deep stroking and James' ass spasmed and fluttered at the memory, aching with the hollow feeling the loss of those talented fingers left behind. A grunt of frustration escaped his swollen lips.

James felt his T-shirt being rolled up his torso, exposing his back to the cold, hard bricks pressing in from behind. Cool night air chilled the beads of sweat on his chest and his nipples crinkled in response to the sudden temperature change. Once the shirt had reached his underarms, large, warm hands explored his naked body, pinching and coarsely massaging over his tender flesh.

Still pressed hips to shoulders against the wall,

legs forced wide by a thick, muscular thigh, jeans unbuttoned and halfway down his naked hips, James reeled, overwhelmed by the thrill and the danger of having sex with an unfamiliar lover in a public place. The threat of possible discovery heightened his lust, and the need to touch skin became too urgent to deny. He moaned at the continued assault on his earlobe and torso, and strained against the restrictive embrace, hands coming up to scrabble at the buttons of the man's shirt.

The fevered sucking at his neck disappeared and the weight of the cowboy's body pressed warningly into his own, forcing a grunt of discomfort from him. The same hands delighting him only seconds ago, now ,encircled his wrists and slammed them to the wall by his shoulders. Shaken, James peered up to see pale blue eyes staring intently down at him from only a few inches away. They narrowed, then relaxed, just as the grip on his wrists did the same. James couldn't stop the tremor of fear that shot down his spine.

"I'll tell you when you can touch."

His wrists were released and a hand ran down the side of his lean frame, petting and soothing as it stroked. His body shook again, this time in anticipation.

"I told you, I like it when you tremble under me."

The large hands skated back up his arms and pressed his wrists into the bricks.

James closed his eyes and melted against the wall, waiting for the man's next move. His hips were yanked forward, the pressure easing off his lower half and both of the cowboy's hands slid inside the back of his jeans. Strong fingers kneaded and rubbed the fleshiest part of his small, firm ass. Occasionally, a thumb would slip down the crease, teasing at the tight ring of muscle nestled there.

His mouth was reclaimed and James lost himself in the rhythm. The hands became more frenzied, mauling and bruising in their strength, and the kiss turned into an attack, the man's mouth devouring, fierce and unrelenting.

James' eyes flashed open and a near breathless gasp tore out of his burning lungs as the assault moved downward. His jeans were shoved to his knees, his hips pinned back in place, bare backside grinding into the sharp edges of the gritty wall. His hard, jutting cock was engulfed in a sleeve of unbearable heat, swallowed to the root and held motionless there. His tormentor made no effort to do the usual blowjob gestures, holding perfectly still and forcing James to do the same. James ached with the need to move.

His fists pounded uselessly on the surface behind him. "Fucking bastard! *Do* something."

The sudden swirl of slick, hot fluid around his rod took him by surprise.

The cowboy swished and swirled a mouthful of spit around like a morning gargle of mouthwash, sucking and releasing, surging the slick liquid against James' most sensitive part again and again. He forced the body-hot fluid up to tease the underside of the delicate tip before he swallowed several times, milking James' cock like a cow's udder. James gave a strangled cry and grabbed frantically at cowboy's head, settling both hands in his hair. Cowboy instantly stopped and stood up, prompting a distressed gasp from James.

Once again James found his entire body pinned against the wall, wrists held to his sides. Warm breath poured down his neck as the man purred a low, sultry threat in his ear.

"Bad boy. Told you not to touch. I see I'm going to have to find another way to make you listen."

Unable to catch his breath, James could only pant and stare. His stare turned wide-eyed as the rolled shirt under his arms was yanked up and off, his head freed, but his arms still encased in the knit fabric. It was pulled down as far as his hands, then the bulk of the shirt was bunched and twisted, locking his wrists in a tight vice of soft cloth. Before he could protest, the length between his wrists was forced over his head to rest behind his neck, effectively pinning his hands at his shoulders. Once again, he was pressed into the cold wall, the skin of his back scraping over the uneven stone.

"What the hell is this shit?"

"This is me," the cowboy leaned in the last inch and nipped James' lower lip, the swollen flesh throbbing at the sharp sting, "forcing you," another bite to his upper lip forced a small grunt of pain from him, "to do what I tell you to do."

The firm, demanding mouth crushed James' swollen lips, the kiss fierce and possessive, startling and more than a little frightening. James began to wonder if coming out into this alley had been a good idea after all. A feeling of helplessness settled over him, disturbing and thrilling at the same time. Unable to do anything else, he gave into the kiss, relaxing back against the wall and into the hard frame grinding against his now mostly naked body.

A sudden flare of arousal shot through him and he groaned into the mouth devouring his, his body arching into the warm hands roughly rubbing and pinching at his nipples. Once erect, coarse fingers plucked at the swollen nubs of flesh, twisting them just past the point of pleasure.

Fingernails flicked at their heated peaks, sending shock waves of burning, painful delight straight to his neglected groin.

Abruptly, all the warmth, weight and stimulation were gone, leaving James conscious of how naked and exposed he really was. Gasping at the abrupt loss, he opened his eyes to look into his lover's face. Instead of the sight of his captor, his world turned 180 degrees and his gaze met only bricks, his chest now pressed into the wall that had been behind him. The full weight of his larger companion returned, the man's physical power both reassuring and overwhelming in its force. James turned his head and muffled a cry of pain into the twisted fabric binding his wrists, the cowboy's weight forcing his straining erection to rest against the cold, irregular surface of the wall.

"Ready yet, baby?" A hot column of flesh slid between the crack of his ass, rubbing up and down, to dip snuggly between his thighs. "Want me?" James' cock was encased in a sandpaper-lined sheath of heat and muscle as the cowboy worked him into a higher state of need with one hand. "Come on, baby, talk to me. Tell me you want it. Tell me that tight, little ass of yours is screaming for me to shove myself home. 'Cause that's what your ass is, baby, home. Tight, hot, home. It belongs to me now. You belong to me now. Don't you, baby?"

A faint buzz of unease rang in his head, but before James could track it down, the talented hand on his erection tightened, almost painful in its strength. The cowboy's thumb began to rub the underside and top of his rod, massaging the drops of leaking fluid into the sensitive skin. The man rubbed his face over James' sweaty, tangled hair and inhaled deeply. All other thoughts fled from his mind as teeth bit at the soft area behind his ear and a wet tongue invaded its outer shell. James bucked into the brutal grip, a groan of need and passion escaping him.

"I'll take that as a 'yes'."

There was the crackle of foil and a small moan from behind him then James' legs were kicked apart and a thigh forced one of his legs up a few inches. Cool air caressed the exposed opening to his body for a brief instant until it was replaced with a blunt heat. A deep grunt and the cowboy invaded him, shoving past the protective ring of muscle to bury his thickness to the hilt in one powerful surge of lust and possessive desire.

Grateful his ass wasn't new to anal intercourse, James screamed into the shirt, biting down on a wad of fabric to muffle the cry. The hand on his cock tightened and sped up, working his softening erection back to full, aching engorgement. Cowboy began to pound into him, his thrusts deep and relentless, torturing James with the force of his strength and the full length of his cock. Each deep stroke nudged at the rings of muscles guarding his deepest reaches. The rarely touched nerve endings buzzed and tingled, making him gasp and writhe against the cowboy. Pinned between rock hard flesh and unyielding brick, James was helpless to do more than flex his lower body's muscles in rhythm to the cowboy's brutal thrusts.

Mindless of the abrasions marking his front, James ground himself into the assault, pitching over the edge to climax as one particularly ambitious thrust breached his inner ring of muscle. A heavy strike of his head on the rough brick forced his face into the shirt's fabric, cutting off his strangled cry. The hand on his cock continued to work him mercilessly, pulling every last drop from him, dragging him over the edge of pleasure into the realm of over-stimulated pain as the grip increased.

His gasping and bucking turned from a passionate response to one of achieving release from his tormentor's unrelenting attentions. His struggle seemed to heighten the cowboy's pleasure and the thrusts into his body intensified. James could feel the fullness in his ass growing and his body spasmed around the thickness, tightening and responding to it, despite James' panic.

The raw soreness at his groin took on a sharper edge. Small, almost elusive thrills of pleasure began to replace the chaffing tugs of the callused hand. His erection began to return, spurred on by the addition of the cowboy's other hand, caressing and fondling lower, rolling his tightening sac and applying a teasing pressure to the stretched skin beneath.

The distant sound of a brief argument down the alley reminded James of the possibility of discovery and he groaned and shuddered, the tremor running the length of his tense, exhausted frame. The low, throaty voice vibrated at the base of his ear lobe, coming in short, electrifying pants that pushed James' excitement even higher.

"That's it, that's it. Tremble for me, baby. I'll give you what you need. I'll take you as rough as you can stand. Fucking *shake* for me, baby."

James was suddenly lifted higher, his boots losing contact with the gritty street, his entire body supported by the cowboy and the wall. The shift in position changed the angle of entry and the pounding thrusts began to skate mercilessly across his prostate. Half a dozen thrusts later he screamed silently into his bound wrists, the climax so painfully intense and unexpected he couldn't find the breath to give voice to his agonized pleasure.

His body rigid, locked in a spasm of peaking climax, James felt every inch of his lover's cock embedded deep inside, its pulsing heat emptying into him at a furious rate. Heavy groans and muttered oaths were lost in the fabric around his neck, still binding his hands in place. The large hands that had caressed and fondled him now held him by the hips, impaling him motionless on the shaft, creating bruised indentations in his tender flesh. He rode out the storm of passion, and then collapsed, wanting to rest against the chill of the bricks to help revive his flagging energy and awareness. An empty, hollow ache replaced the shrinking iron rod inside of him, and chill air drifted over his back and buttocks as his partner stepped away.

In a half stupor, cheek resting on the rough brick surface, he felt his pants pulled up around his hips and his arms were slowly lowered. The thin fabric of his shirt was unrolled and worked up his arms, slipped down over his head, then tugged and smoothed until it covered his body.

James pushed off of the wall, but was spun and pinned back against it before he could turn on his own power. Gentle, but demanding lips captured his and he lost track of time as the cowboy's tongue reacquainted itself with every molecule in his mouth. The large body settled over him, strong arms embracing him, re-igniting his earlier unease with the possessive stranger.

Breaking off the kiss, James pushed at the man's shoulders until the tight arms released him. He quickly stepped to one side and fastened the buttons down the front of his jeans, aware of the other man watching his hands as they worked.

"Well, ah, that was terrific. Thanks. I, ah, it was

fantastic, really. But I have to get going. Work in the morning. Maybe we'll run into each other again sometime."

James stepped to one side to walk around the cowboy, but was forced to halt when the man matched his movement.

"Look, my truck is right here." Cowboy pointed at the late model, extended cab, monster of a truck James had noticed earlier. It was parked only a few yards down the alley, facing the other end, a convenient spot for leaving unseen by the bar's patrons. "I'll drive you to your car." Cowboy herded James toward the truck, hands tucked unthreateningly in his pants' pockets, a smile of shy delight on his rugged face.

James hesitated for a moment, but decided against making a scene. He allowed the cowboy to open the driver's door for him, the passenger side parked too close to the wall to go around. Reaching up for a handhold on the truck's raised interior, a pair of too helpful hands grabbed his waist.

"Then again, maybe I'll just take you home. Tying you to my bed sounds like the perfect way to end the night."

James was lifted into the air and tossed across the bench seat. He sprawled against the far door. By the time he regained his footing, the cowboy was seated behind the wheel and the door was shut and locked.

James gathered his adrenaline-spiked energy and launched himself at the man. The cowboy's head thudded against the window and his tall body bowed under James' weight. James almost managed to grab the door handle before his wrists were engulfed in the cowboy's large, work-rough palms. One swift, shifting move of Cowboy's hips and James found himself pinned on his back to the truck's bench seat. Cowboy hovered over him, holding James' wrists to either side of his head.

"Hey, hey. Slow down there, Tiger. It was a joke, just a joke. Okay?" The same soft voice that had thrilled and delighted James only moments ago rumbled in his ear again. This time the voice was warm and conciliatory instead of dark and demanding. Oddly enough, James responded to it in the same thrilled way, feeling a burst of attraction run down his spine. The sensation made James shudder and *that* made Cowboy smile. To James, it was a dazzling, heart-stopping smile.

"Still trembling under me, huh?" Cowboy chuckled and released James' wrists, but didn't move. Cowboy's smile softened and his expression changed from playful to sincere. "I still like that, but I didn't mean to scare you."

Cowboy ran his thumb across James' panting mouth, his gaze riveted to the swollen, flushed lips. He glanced up to catch James' own heated gaze and the smile changed again, this time to shy. "I'm very pleased to meet you." Cowboy winked, then heaved himself up, bringing James along with him.

"Ah, hi. I'm James, James Justin." James smoothed down his rumpled shirt then extended his hand. "Nice to meet you, too." Cowboy shook his hand and grinned.

The man's appreciative, lopsided smile made James feel suddenly desirable all over again, the fantastic ache in his ass re-ignited as his stretched and used opening spasmed. Flustered by the strong pull of attraction for the big man, James settled as close to the passenger door as he could. His thoughts were thick and sluggish, still overwhelmed by the lingering euphoria from their earlier coupling.

James didn't want to mistake lust for real attraction, but something about this cowboy made him want more, more time with the man, more conversations, more sex, definitely, more sex. Although James wanted all those things,he wanted to be sure this would be about more than *just* sex.

Feeling awkward and suddenly adolescent, James gave an embarrassed chuckle. "Actually, it was better than nice. It was absolutely-fucking-fabulous."

James thought he detected a faint blush on the man's tanned and weathered face. Cowboy laughed softly. "I won't argue with that."

The laughter tapered off into what threatened to become an awkward silence. Cowboy shoved the key into the ignition and started the truck, glancing over at James as he did it. "I'm headed for my favorite coffee shop. Want to come along?" Cowboy let the truck idle at the mouth of the alley.

James gestured to the left and they turned onto a quiet side street. Surprised by the offer, James stammered, "Ah, thanks." He looked at the digital clock on the dashboard and sighed. "But I have to be to work in a few hours. I need to get some sleep." He pointed out the windshield at the row of parked cars. "The black Vibe is mine."

Cowboy pulled up beside the sleek little Vibe. He put his own truck into park, ignoring a sedan and two motorcycles that were forced to go around them. "Okay then." He sounded impatient and he tapped the steering wheel with the fingers of one hand, glancing repeatedly in the rearview mirror.

Thinking the display meant the cowboy had already lost interest, James opened the door and slid from the truck. He felt his face flame with the sudden uncomfortable flush of shame at being discarded so quickly. Just as he was about to shut the door, the cowboy called out to him.

"Hey, Jamie?"

Startled by the intimate nickname, James swung the door back open to find the cowboy leaning low across the seat. The position brought the big man eye-to-eye with James. The lopsided grin was back on Cowboy's face.

"How about dinner tomorrow night?"

Stunned by the invitation, James slowly nodded his head. He was momentarily frozen in place by the intensity of the thrill that rolled through the pit of his stomach then spread south.

"Yeah. Yeah, we could do that. Seven o'clock?"

Actions hidden from public view by the truck seat and dashboard, Cowboy reached out one long arm and laced the fingers of his massive hand through the hair at the back of James' head. He tugged, drawing James forward to lean into the cab, where cowboy delivered a blistering kiss. When he released James, it was only a fraction of an inch, his lips still brushing over James' tingling mouth as he panted out an order. "Six."

Throwing reason out the window, James grabbed cowboy by the hair with both hands and sealed his mouth to the willing lips, eagerly returning the attention. When James pulled back, they were both breathless and flushed. "Six. Okay."

The fingers in his hair loosened and James backed out of the truck. The cowboy straightened up behind the wheel. James' gaze fell on the bright digital clock display on the dash again and he panicked.

His right hand sliced the air, going between him

and the dashboard several times in a row. He shifted his weight from leg to leg, a slight bounce punctuating each move. "Ah, is that tonight's tonight or tomorrow's tonight? It's one-thirty. I mean, it's after midnight. I mean, it's already Saturday. Did you mean -- ."

A snort of amusement cut off his sentence. James looked up from the clock display, startled, to meet the other man's delighted expression.

"I like it when you're flustered," said the cowboy. He chuckled then lowered his voice to a sultry tone adding, "It makes me want to direct all that energy you're putting out into more 'relaxing' activities."

James felt his blood rushing both north and south, leaving him dizzy. His face turned a bright red, and blood pooled in his groin, coaxing his cock partially awake. He ducked his head, suddenly shy with this man who had just spent the last half an hour turning his brains to mush by way of his ass.

"Jamie?" It was only one word, whispered in the cowboy's rough, low voice, but it eased James' embarrassment.

He raised his head to met Cowboy's eyes, relieved to see gentle understanding in the man's face, as well as sexual interest. The thread of excitement rolling through his stomach turned into a large ball of warm, sizzling electricity.

"Six o'clock tonight. Saturday. s in sixteen and a half-hours from now, okay?" Cowboy pulled a business card out from the edge of the truck's sun visor and held it out to James. "That's my cell number printed at the bottom. Call me later today and give me directions to your place."

Wishing he had more time to think about the

situation without offending the cowboy, James took it. He glanced at the printing, noting the construction firm advertised on the card. It was a very well known, highly recommended company. Even the architectural firm he worked for did business with them. It was nice to know the cowboy had a solid job. James hated to think he might end up falling for a deadbeat.

"That way you can have time to think about things," said Cowboy.

James bit his lower lip, a guilty little snort escaping.

Cowboy just smiled. "I'm feeling a little flushed with myself right now, too. Once your blood decides to visit your brain again, you can decide if you want to call. Then if you want to back out, you won't have given your home address to someone you don't want to see outside of an alley."

James struggled not to let the grin trying to break free out, but lost. "I've pretty much decided I'd like to see you anywhere, even another alley."

Nodding, Cowboy settled more comfortably behind the wheel. "All right then. We've got a date."

A car full of drunken young men honking their horn and tossing obscenities in the air flew by, and then disappeared around a corner.

Cowboy gestured one big hand toward James' parked car. "You get in. I'll wait here until you pull out." He winked at James. "I've got a vested interest in making sure you stay safe."

James snorted and shut the truck door. Pocketing the card in his front pants pocket, James couldn't resist running his fingertips over the half-hard bulge tucked up against the rough denim of his jeans. The small gesture started the lingering buzz to tingle again. As he turned to open his car door, he gave one last look over his shoulder. Cowboy sat silently watching him.

James yanked his hand out of his pants and slid into his car, closing and locking the door before starting it. He eased the car from curb, experiencing a moment of panic when the truck followed him for two blocks. Just when James began to think he might have a stalker on his hands, the truck took a right turn and sped off toward an older, quieter section of the city.

James drove two more blocks, basking in the thrill of reliving the unexpected, erotic adventure in the alleyway, before he realized he hadn't asked the Cowboy his name.

Chapter Two

Finding a name above the printed cell number on the business card, James had ignored the butterflies assaulting his stomach, and called mid-morning. The moment he heard the cowboy's low, sultry voice answer, the butterflies had flown straight to his cock and danced on its rapidly engorging head.

He pressed the phone tighter to his ear, slightly confused by the loud background noises until he remembered the cowboy worked a construction site. James forced himself to concentrate on Cowboy's words.

"Bram Lord. What can I do for you?"

James felt his stomach tighten with excitement. "Ah, Bram, hi. It's me, James, from last night. You said to call. So I'm, ah, calling."

The background noise became muffled and the reception suddenly got clearer. James mentally pictured the big man in full denim garb and a hard hat, gritty with concrete dust and sweat streaking his tanned, chiseled face The thought of the phone tucked to the side of his face as leather work gloves smoothed his rough hands as various tools hung from Cowboy's belt, completed James' fantasy.

He had to reach down the front of his pants and shift his aching erection to a more comfortable position or risk talking an octave above normal for the rest of the conversation.

James didn't think it was possible but the man's

voice got even sexier.

"Jamie!"

The one word was said with so much genuine pleasure James blushed.

Bram continued, "I'm really glad you decided to call. I've been kicking myself all morning for being so chivalrous last night. I would have called you over breakfast. Or called you over to have breakfast."

Pleased by Bram's willingness to reveal his continuing attraction so easily, James took courage from the admission.

"I don't eat breakfast, but thanks for the thought. If tonight is still a go, you'll need my address." A slight pause on the other end of the line made James' heart skip a beat. "Unless you've changed your mind?"

"What? Hell, no, Jamie. Dinner is on. Six o'clock. I was just searching for a piece of paper. To write your address on." There was the rustle of paper and Bram's voice faded for a moment, like he was switching hands with the phone. "Don't want to make any mistakes and show up late. I hate being late." Bram's voice sounded closer, like he had pressed the mouthpiece to his face. "Shoot, Tiger, I'm ready for you."

The last was said with a bit more sultriness. James had a visual of the big man naked and hard, broad muscles oiled and flexed, one massive, rough palm soothing up and down his straining cock, while the other hand gestured to James to come closer. A husky whisper proclaimed, "I'm ready for you."

James gasped at the rush of blood that filled his cock then fumbled with the phone when the sultry come-on was repeated in his ear. This time Bram sounded perplexed.

"I'm ready for you. Jamie? I know you're still there, I can hear you panting. You okay?"

James bit his lower lip hard, letting the pain distract his soaring libido. He winced when a tooth cut into a small crack in his chapped lip. "Owe. Yeah, yeah, I'm fine, fine. Ah, someone just . . . stopped by my office for second. I got distracted by you -- them, them. But you're -- they're gone now."

The warm chuckle James remembered from last night rumbled across the telephone line, losing none of its heat along the way. "Good. I'd hate to think I'd lost your attention already. Now give me your address. I have to get back to work."

"Oh, sorry. I live in the Butler Building on West 12th, apartment 4C, at the end of the hall. You have to be buzzed up, but I should be home in plenty of time before six." James rubbed his thumb over his sore lip. He couldn't decide whether he hoped Bram would shave tonight or not.

"I hope so." The big man's voice took another dive to the deep end of the vocal pool. "Like I said, I'm not fond of late. In my world, late gets you punished."

The implied, playful threat sent a flash of lust and desire burning down every nerve ending in James' body. He felt sweat break out on his skin and a chain reaction of gooseflesh followed. He shivered, almost dropping the phone.

"Punished? What kind of punishment?"

"Whatever fits the crime, fits the criminal. I like to be creative."

"Uh-huh. Ah, um." James swallowed and tried to steady his breathing, his mouth suddenly dry. "Have a lot of practice in that area?"

"Enough."

"Ooookay. I'll just have to be sure I'm not late." James let out a long, shaky breath, knowing it traveled over the phone line. Bram's forcefulness thrilled and attracted James. And it scared him, too.

Bram's tone stayed low and sexy, but the dark edge had disappeared. "I'll see you at six, then. Dress nice, but nothing fancy. No T-shirts. Soon, Jamie."

The line went dead before James could comment or protest. He stared at the silent handset then replaced it in its base. He wasn't used to being given orders about how to dress, but it *was* nice to know what was expected from him.

That was the hardest part of dating for James, understanding a complete stranger's unspoken desires and wants, second-guessing their expectations, and, all too often for James, falling short.

Not that he was having any trouble understanding Bram. The man was very open and obvious about his intentions and his wants. James didn't have to guess at anything the big man was thinking, not since the moment he'd laid eyes on the cowboy. Bram was forceful and straightforward. Both qualities were very appealing to James.

One last frustrated nip at his abused lower lip and James got back to work, trying desperately not to hear the soft, rough "I'm ready for you" whispering in the back of his mind.

***

Shifting his portfolio from his right hand to his left to get out his keys, James juggled the two-foot by three-foot document carrier, trying to make his short fingers wrap around the handles of both his briefcase and it at the same time. He had limited success, only saving them both from dropping to the ground by pressing them tightly to his chest.

The pressure reawakened the burn of the abrasions dotting his torso, a lasting reminder of his first meeting with the man he was rushing home to get ready to see. The small burst of sizzling discomfort shot straight to his groin and James had to drop the portfolio lower to hide his body's response.

He pressed the button for the elevator up to his apartment floor and stepped into the first empty car that appeared, lost in thought over his new relationship.

For the tenth time today, a tiny warning signal flared in the back of his mind reminding him to be cautious. A total stranger, who had no qualms about inflicting physical pain on a new sexual partner, even if it was something the partner wanted, should be approached carefully.

Certainly James had enjoyed the whole scene in the alley, nearly begged for it, was fucking outrageously turned on by it, but he was the one living with the lingering pains.

The abrasions on his body hurt with every brush of his clothing; his ass ached and spasmed when he sat and his lips were chapped raw and swollen from the cowboy's prickly stubble. Even James' cock felt like it had been scoured with sandpaper instead of just the cowboy's work-rough hands. If this cowboy planned on getting any rougher than last night, James would need to defy his growing attraction for the man and avoid him.

But that wouldn't be happening right now.

Stepping off the elevator, James jumped to one side, twisting and spinning to dodge two growling bulldogs on chains. In the effort to avoid coming into mauling range of the snarling, straining animals, James backed into their owner.

"Watch where you're going, punk."

A shove to his shoulder sent James stumbled back to thump against the apartment hallway wall, fumbling for hold on his slipping workload. "Sorry, I didn't see you. The dogs surprised me."

"Afraid of a couple pets, Jamie-boy?"

James straightened up and cast a reluctant glance at the thirty-something man holding the ends of the dog chains. Dressed in military fatigues and boots from the waist down, the square, boxy, but well-muscled man sported a sleeveless T-shirt on his upper torso and a Harley-Davidson handkerchief tied around his thick neck.

"They're not pets, Williams. You train them to pit fight. Everybody knows that." James found a better hold on his briefcase with his left hand and settled the portfolio against the wall.

Williams marched up to James and pushed him until they were chest-to-chest with James pressed onto the wall behind him. James' head thudded against the painted drywall with the force of the impact.

"So what? You going to do something about it, Jamie-boy?" Williams sneered into James' face.

The sour smell of old beer and cigarette smoke made James flinch and turn his head from the stench. He was unnerved, but he didn't believe Williams would do anything extreme in a public hallway, even a deserted one.

"Those dogs shouldn't be allowed in the building,

man. There are little kids living here," said James.

As subtly as possible, James thumbed the keys on his keyring between the fingers of his right hand, slowly creating a making shift weapon to defend himself if the confrontation escalated.

Williams pushed his forearm under James' chin and pressed until James grimaced.

"You going to be their guardian angel, Jamie-boy? Huh?" Williams leaned in and ground himself against the other man, massaging a growing erection over James' hip.

James hissed and swallowed down the bile that rose in his throat. "Get off me, asshole."

"Whoa. Big words, from a sweet little boy." James' vision was suddenly filled with Williams' pitted face as the man leaned in close. "I've been wondering lately just how sweet." He tried to capture James' lips in an open-mouthed kiss.

James responded with a sharp punch to Williams' side, all four keys in his hand extended and braced for maximum effect.

Williams grunted and lifted his groin away, lessening the pressure on James' throat at the same time. But he was toned and firm, and with limited room to swing, James' punch had little effect.

Williams grabbed James' wrist and pinned it to the wall over James' head. James squirmed and twisted, trying to avoid the man's face.

The struggle seemed to excite Williams. "Why you little cocksucker." He laughed and held James' face immobile with the pressure from his arm then leered. "You just might be worth risking the jail time for after all, Jamie-boy."

Williams pressed in harder with both his arm and

his groin until James coughed and bucked against him. James tried to raise the briefcase between them, but Williams knocked it from his hand. It skidded down the hallway to thump against an apartment door.

In the background, the dogs let out several low growls, dancing in place with impatience, the jingle of the heavy chains marking each frenzied step. Williams didn't even turn to look at them. He flashed a hand signal at the animals and grunted a curt, "Stay!" The growls tapered off into high-pitched whines then disappeared altogether.

James saw the raw lust settle over Williams and his mouth went suddenly dry. His restrained wrist was brought closer to his head and James felt the man's fingertips as they wove through his hair and pulled tight.

"Let. Go!" James spit through gritted teeth. "Perverted dick!"

Pulling hard on the handful of curls, Williams tilted James' face up. "Who's going to save your sweet ass, Jamie-boy?" James closed his eyes tightly as Williams' ugly, leering face drew near.

"I guess that would be me."

James felt Williams freeze in place. It took a full five seconds before James realized the soft, husky voice near his ear hadn't come from his attacker.

Williams never got the chance to realize much of anything. He was ripped off James' chest and slammed face first into the wall, again and again. Blood from his nose splattered the wall in increasing amounts until it left a surreal imprint of the man's face on the pastel-colored surface.

James dropped, panting, to one knee, amazed at the sight before him. Bram towered over Williams, manhandling the molester with an ease and power that rocked James. The cowboy had Williams reduced to a battered heap of useless muscle and brawn in under twenty seconds.

When Williams finally hit the floor, one of the dogs broke his training, jumping over James' kneeling body to launch himself at his master's attacker. Bram blocked the snapping jaws, pinned the snarling animal with his knees and deftly snapped the dog's neck, letting the quivering body fall to the floor by Williams. The other dog paced and whined, but stayed put.

Trembling from the rush of adrenaline and fear, James pushed himself to his feet. He used one hand to brace himself on the wall while the other rubbed his reddened throat. James hopped over the fallen bodies, stumbling a little when he miscalculated a step. Bram caught him by the arm.

"Do we need an ambulance here?"

James shook his head and coughed, massaging at the ache in his throat. "Only for him." He gestured at his fallen attacker.

Williams was just beginning to come back to his senses. He moaned and pushed himself up to a sitting position against the wall, feebly wiping at the blood flowing from his misshapen nose.

"Fat chance of that happening." Bram slipped an arm around James' shoulders and began to pry the keys from James' white-knuckled hand. "Loosen up, Tiger. He's down."

James huffed out a surprised breath and watched the cowboy unbend his own stiff, numb fingers. Once the keys were free, Bram pocketed them. He touched James' quivering shoulder and said, "Stay right here."

Numb, James barely nodded.

Grabbing the fallen portfolio, Bram crouched beside a subdued Williams.

Williams flinched, but recovered enough bravado to attempt a half-hearted sneer. "Who the hell are you, Jamie-boy's new bodyguard?"

"No, his new boyfriend, his very possessive, protective boyfriend. You might want to remember that from now on." Bram started to rise then stopped and leaned closer to Williams. "And one other thing."

Bram's hand shot out and grabbed Williams by the neck, pinning him against the wall. Williams' neck was as thick as a tree trunk, but Bram had no trouble gripping it.

"Don't ever, *ever* call him 'Jamie' again," said Bram. Williams gasped and tried to pull free, but the grip only tightened. "Got it?"

Williams gurgled an unintelligible reply and nodded.

Bram released his hold, wiping his bloodied hand off on Williams' white T-shirt. Standing, he shoved the dog's dead body out of his way with one foot and walked back over to a shivering James.

"Let's get you inside. You're hurt." Bram herded James down the hallway to his door.

"Not really." James' voice broke on the last word, his abused vocal cords betraying him. He ducked his head whispering, "Well, okay. Maybe just a little."

"Uh-huh. I can hear that 'just a little'." Opening the apartment with James' keys, Bram pocketed the keyring again and locked the door behind them.

"Do you want to call the police, Jamie?"

James snorted in disgust. "No. All they'll see is Williams' broken nose and dead dog. We'll be lucky if William's doesn't call them on us."

Bram gave a mirthless chuckle. "And report he got beat up by a gay man? I don't think so. By tonight that jerk'll be telling his buddies about how he got his nose broke in some spectacular bar fight where he laid out six bikers."

After a quick glance around the tidy, well-furnished space, Bram placed James' work materials on an architect's drawing table standing in the middle of the room. "Has he bothered you before?"

"Not really." James sighed and waved a hand vaguely in the air. "A few remarks when I've been coming in at night and our paths have crossed." He stopped and stared into the distance for a moment. "Come to think of it, he's been in the hall a lot lately. He kind of stares at me, so I never do anything to invite conversation." James snorted a broken chuckle. "I'm sure not talking to him after this."

A wave of nausea rolled through his stomach and James reached out for the wall to steady himself and found Bram there instead. The big man guided James over to sit on the couch.

"No. No, I . . . I need to . . . don't want to sit. Not right now." James slipped from Bram's light grip and began to pace the room, randomly fussing with small items on the shelves and tables, then ducking into the compact kitchen area off the living room and back out again.

Bram occupied himself with looking over the plans on the drawing table. "I recognize this. It's on the East Side of town. A historical restoration isn't it?"

James stuck his head out of the kitchen. "Yeah, a huge one, The Becker Estate. The architectural firm I work for was asked to design and oversee the work." James sighed and shook his head. "I thought for sure I'd be given the project. That era is my area of expertise. I love it. I've been working on these plans, on my own time, for six months. Ever since I heard it was a possibility." He leaned against the kitchen door jab then pushed abruptly off it. "They gave it to a senior architect on Friday." James turned and walked back out of the room. "I need a drink of . . . something."

Bram studied the layers of technical drawings more closely. He called out over his shoulder as he thumbed through the pile. "Did they see these? Before they made the decision who to give it to?"

"No." James wandered back into the living, hands still empty. "I was all ready to present them to my boss, then Art Wheeler told me he'd been 'saddled' with it. He's one of the senior architects I mentioned. Didn't seem to be any point in showing them to anyone after that."

"It's a shame for all this work to go to waste, Jamie. It's brilliant. You should show them to someone anyway. It couldn't hurt."

"Maybe." Frowning, James made a helpless gesture with his hands in the air. "I'll make us some coffee. I could use coffee. Yeah, I'll make . . .coffee." James shrugged off his jacket then put it back on, rubbing his arms. "Kinda cold in here." He gave a dry, embarrassed chuckle and disappeared into the kitchen again. He popped back out to ask, "Do you want coffee?"

"Sure, unless you've got something stronger." Slipping off his long, Western style, leather overcoat and tossing it on a chair, Bram sat down and watched the younger man's increasingly frantic movements.

James knelt down by an old oak cabinet. "I think I have a bottle of brandy in here. A Christmas present from the boss, Mr. Dunn. Good brandy, too. Except, I don't drink much and never alone. Drinking's kind of a purely social thing for me. Loosens me up to talk. And if there's no one to talk to, what's the point of drinking in the first place, you know?"

James pulled a bottle from the back of the cabinet and started to stand. A wave of dizziness washed over him. James felt the room tilt and grow dim, then black.

After the room had righted itself, James found himself cradled against Bram, both of them lying on the couch. James was draped over Bram and Bram's leather coat was draped over James, the big man's arms holding him securely in place.

Looking up into the pale blue eyes studying him intently, James blushed, suddenly feeling like a fainting damsel in distress from a corny soap opera.

"God, I'm so sorry about all this." James pushed himself up on trembling arms and Bram helped him to sit up. James missed the warmth immediately. Shivers raced down his spine.

Bram smiled his lopsided, playful grin. "I don't know. It hasn't been a total loss. I still got the chance to feel you tremble again."

James snorted a panic-tinged laugh. "I liked the reasons for it better last night." He puffed out two breathes in rapid succession to calm himself. "I don't want to ever go through what happened in the hallway again."

He suddenly needed space between himself and the huge man hovering beside him. He jumped up and fled to the other side of the room, taking refuge behind the drafting table, relieved when Bram made no move to follow.

James gave Bram an apologetic shrug and whispered, "I don't like being scared. I don't want to be hurt, either." Nervous, James ran his hand up and down the edge of table as he talked. "I like forceful, but not being forced, you know?"

"Yeah, Jamie, I do. I know the difference." Bram relaxed back against the cushions, running a hand through his honey-blond hair, leaving it tousled and spiky on one side.

James found the look endearing. He realized the big man was working hard at looking as non-threatening as possible, staying seated, giving James his space. He wandered a few steps out from behind the table.

"Yeah? You know the difference?" James couldn't keep the note of hope from his voice.

"Yeah." Bram nodded solemnly. "Jamie, I would *never* treat you the way that bone-headed asshole just did. I said I like it when you tremble against me, and it's no lie. I do. But I want it to be with excitement, desire, or frustration and need, and yeah, maybe a little fear. But fear from not knowing how I'm going to blow your mind next -- with pleasure. Not from fear of being hurt or of being forced to do something you don't want." Bram touched his chest and lowered his voice to just above a whisper. "I'm not like that."

"Yeah?" James advanced a few more tentative feet toward the couch. A small smile tugged at his lips. "You plan on 'blowing my mind' any time soon?"

"*Yeah.*" Bram chuckled, a leering smile tweaked at the corner of his mouth. "I have all kinds of plans for 'soon'."

Bram looked James over from head to toe and back again. "Come here, baby." He patted the couch cushion.

James slowly advanced the last few paces to the couch and sat down. He was immediately engulfed in warmth as Bram wrapped his arms and his coat around James' shoulders. The same scent of leather and sweat from the alleyway filled James' head. He felt a slight responsive stirring in his groin, a pleasant lick of flame waiting to be coaxed to life.

Suddenly very tired, James relaxed into the welcome comfort. He found himself leaning into Bram's offered support, his cheek coming to rest on the expansive, hard chest under his head.

"Just rest, Tiger. You're going to be all right." Bram's rough-soft, understanding tone brought tears to James' eyes.

Bram threaded the fingers of one hand through James' curls and rubbed lightly over the spot where Williams had yanked on his hair, soothing the lingering ache.

James felt a surge of something he could only describe as 'right' buzz through him. Being with this big, gentle, but commanding man felt. . . good, very, very good. Tears began to burn at the back of his eyes again. James had to close them to chase away the threat.

Bram's arm was around him and the big man's hand rested easily on James' slender hip. Bram began a light stroking motion over the curve, brushing gently back and forth.

The soothing gesture started a tingling sensation to bloom in James. That was when he discovered his cock had a direct connection with any part of his body Bram touched. It stirred and stretched seemingly seeking out the source of stimulation, trying to direct the attention to itself.

Deciding to trust his gut instincts about this stranger, James turned in Bram's hold and leaned up, studying the other man's reaction as he came in close. Encouraged by the quiet, patient expression in Bram's eyes, James slowly touched his lips to the other man's open, waiting mouth.

The shame and fear from earlier melted away, replaced with raw, blinding need. Need to be held, need to be touched by someone who wanted to give pleasure, as well as receive it. James needed this moment.

He knew Bram's reaction now would set the tone for their whole relationship. If the man rejected him, disgusted after what Williams had tried to do, James would have to end it here.

Or worse, if the big man decided James was weak, easy prey, and tried to overwhelm him with physical force, the outcome would have to be the same. And James would have to give up the most alluring, satisfying man he had ever met.

Lips trembling, James increased the pressure of the kiss, sliding the tip of his tongue across Bram's lower lip. Tentative, he sucked on the moist, plump flesh, raking his teeth lightly over its sensitive lining, waiting for a response from his partner.

Bram stayed as still as stone and James heart began the slow plunge to his stomach. Just as he was breaking away from what he thought was their last kiss, strong arms embraced him and pulled him up close. Bram slid his hand into James hair and held his mouth in place, devouring James in a slow, primal kiss. James felt like the room had dissolved away, the level of energy and intensity radiating off his lover engulfing him. James let it, returning the kiss with a needy hunger of his own.

Without breaking the kiss, James crawled up Bram's body and the man shifted so they were once more lying on the couch, James on top. Bram's one hand was still anchored in James' hair. The other stroked down his spine in a heavy caress until it reached his ass. There, the greedy digits work his flesh, dividing their time between stroking down the crack of his ass and kneading his firm cheeks.

Bram broke the kiss long enough to mumble against James' lips. "You sure?"

James darted down to suck on Bram's clean-shaven chin, and tongued the small cleft he found there, then licked his way back up to Bram's panting lips. "I'm sure. You sure?"

James dove back in to capture Bram's mouth, but his lover pulled his head back so they were eye-to-eye instead. Bram's expression was soft and serious. He stroked his thumb over James' high-boned cheek, his touch startlingly tender. "I always was."

James' breath hitched and something in his chest spasmed and uncurled, but he wasn't given any time to contemplate all the meanings of Bram's confession. The other man pressed James firmly against him, the force of one large hand drove James' hips down to rub his full erection over Bram's hip. James moved one knee between Bram's legs and brushed over the growing bulge straining against the man's zipper.

Occupied with exploring every cell of Bram's mouth, James was startled when flesh met warm flesh as Bram slid his hand down the inside of the back of James' pants. James gasped, losing the advantage in the battle of tongues in which he was engaged . The gasp faded into a moan when Bram began to suck on James' tongue, matching the rhythm of the stroking fingertips over James' opening.

Groaning out his frustration, James pushed back against the teasing finger. His hands laced deep into Bram's hair and held on while he rocked frantically back and forth, straining to satisfy both his aching cock and his ready asshole.

His need for more stimulation reached a frenzied peak and just when James thought he'd explode if he didn't come, one long, thick, delightfully abrasive finger slid into his ass. James moaned his pleasure into Bram's mouth with a series of rapid, breathless grunts and bucked against the man's hard body. The finger in his ass twisted and turned, torturing the sensitive nerve endings just inside the opening. The rough, callous finger stroked and rubbed, but never plunged deep enough to satisfy.

James tried to tear his mouth away to voice a protest, but Bram wouldn't allow it. The big man held James' lips tightly to his own and renewed the energy of the kiss, ravaging James' mouth, biting his lips, sucking at his tongue and exploring the sensitive roof of his mouth.

Overloaded with sensation, James grew dizzy. His pleas for more were reduced to muffled grunts and moans, each huffed out in time to the frenzied thrusts of his lower body. James nearly wept with the need for release when the teasing finger in his ass plunged deeper and stayed there, high in his passage, swirling again and again over and around the soft, spongy nub of his prostate.

The effect on James was like an electric shock. Every nerve ending sizzled and sparked, his orgasm racing through him in uncontrolled waves of white-lightening pleasure while his body spasmed and rocked in his lover's arms.

When Bram finally released his mouth, James

collapsed down on the man, boneless and breathless, more sated and content than he would have thought possible an hour ago.

"You okay, baby?"

James nodded and buried his forehead in the crook of Bram's neck, trying to get his breathing under control, pulling in shallow gasps of air in rapid succession. Each breath burned his dry, swollen throat, but James didn't care. He'd just had the best orgasm of his life with a man who knew what he needed and was willing to give it to him. James felt wonderful.

Shifting into a more comfortable position, James' leg brushed over the still hard bulge in Bram's pants. Bram's cock strained upward, tenting the fabric with an impressive display of length and girth. James rubbed his knee up the length of it, sitting up enough to smile seductively down at his lover.

"You promised me dinner. I'll skip the salad and start with the main course." James shimmied down Bram's long body, and settled on his knees beside the couch. Bram angled his hips so one leg dropped off the couch and James snuggled in between Bram's thighs, busy hands working Bram's belt and zipper open.

"Jamie, you don't have to. I can wait."

"'Having to' has nothing to do with this." James stepped out of his own soiled pants and boxers, then pulled at Bram's.

Bram lifted his hips off the couch and helped slip the clothing down until it pooled on the floor at his ankles. He toed off his shoes and kicked his pants aside, then relaxed back onto the cushions and seductively spread his legs, pulling up his shirttails to expose himself. He arched his pelvis up, displaying his engorged shaft.

James slid his hands along the panes of Bram's muscular thighs, kneading the warm, hairy flesh, and studied his objective. The head of Bram's penis was shiny with pre-cum, a bead of white resting in the valley of its slit. It sat high enough in the air that James would have to kneel up completely to take it into his mouth. The shaft was ridged and lined with bulging veins. He could see a pulse hammering just under the lip of the head. It was thick enough that James doubted he could swallow it. The head was a deep red, the entire rod enflamed and engorged, vibrating with a need so great it actually swayed to and fro, like a hand beckoning James nearer.

Resisting the tempting call, James ran his fingers down the creases where Bram's thighs met his groin, lightly teasing the coarse hairs and sensitive tissue. He worked one hand into the dense pelt of light brown hair surrounding the base of Bram's cock, exploring and rubbing until his fingers wrapped around the stiff base.

James ran his thumb up the underside of the tense organ and whispered, "God, Bram, you're beautiful."

A sudden gasp from above drew James' gaze upward and he locked on his lover's face, taking pride in the flush now highlighting Bram's tanned cheeks.

Bram panted then moaned, "Never heard that before. Most just bitch about the size."

"No bitching here. I think last night proved it's a perfect fit for me." James had moved closer so each word sent a puff of hot breath over the moist, straining cock head. The big man moaned and arched up. James let the tip rub over his face, but refused to allow it entrance into his mouth.

James' other hand wormed beneath the full, tight sac nestled between Bram's thighs and began rolling it between his palm and fingers. Hands gripped his head and massaged his scalp. The grip was firm, but it didn't pull or shove. James let the warm, coarse palms act as his guide in gauging his new lover's needs.

Dipping his head lower, James nudged Bram's thighs with his chin. The other man slid farther down the cushion and opened his legs wider. James took part of the sac into his mouth, sucking and licking the tightly wrinkled pouch until Bram's ragged panting had turned into one continuous, deep moan.

Releasing the sac, he licked under it, scouring the sensitive strip of ridged flesh leading to Bram's back entrance with his tongue. Just before he reached the puckered hole, James retreated, licking and biting his way back to the base of Bram's quivering cock. James knelt up and brought the thick shaft toward his lips, wanting to taste the droplets of fluid stringing from its opening.

Suddenly hesitant, he looked up to see Bram devouring his every move. "I . . . are you . . . I don't have any . .." James bit his lip. "I'm sorry. I . . ."

"In my pants' pocket. I'm clean, but I know you can't be sure. I just hope you don't mind the taste of latex." Bram dropped his arms to his chest and closed his eyes, panting softly.

James dug through the pile of clothes on the floor and found a roll of condoms, twelve in all. He laughed, pulled one off the roll and tossed the remaining eleven on Bram's chest, startling him.

"Big plans for tonight, lover?" Ripping open the packet, James smoothed the thin sleeve down the length of Bram, working the tight fit over the ridges and bumps until he ran out of condom. "How long was this date going to last?"

Bram plucked the foil wrappers off his sweaty chest and tossed them to one side, panting heavily at the renewed attention to his cock. "Through dinner And dessert and a midnight snack, if I pace it right. Then breakfast, if I'm lucky."

James looked up to catch that seductive, lopsided grin of Bram's. It made him squirm. He gave Bram a half-lidded, sultry look from under his eyelashes and reached down to give his own renewed erection a few lazy strokes. "Maybe you didn't pack enough."

Bram reached down and pulled James up between his out stretched legs to deliver a possessive, blistering kiss that only ended when James moaned. Bram whispered into James' gasping mouth, "Let's find out." Bram pulled his own shirt free and tossed it aside.

James ducked down to take one of Bram's nipples into his mouth. He sucked and rolled the dusky nub until it peaked and blossomed to full life. He worried it with his teeth, tugging and nipping until he could feel the heat radiating from the abused flesh. Then he did the same to the other nipple, his hands soothing and stroking every part of the hard-muscled torso he could reach. He licked his way down the broad chest, following the trail of darkening hairs to bury his face in the mat of fur at the base of Bram's cock.

"Look at me, Jamie. Don't stop looking at me." The deep, commanding voice sent a shiver down his spine and a bead of pre-cum out of his slit.

Glancing up, James locked stares with Bram, thrilled by the way the other man's breathing sped up and his color deepened. Inserting two fingers in his mouth, James lavished them with spit, polishing them with his tongue, putting on a show for his riveted audience of one.

He moved them from his mouth to slide them under Bram's balls, massaging the puckered entrance to his ass. He pushed the tips of his fingers into the hole and stopped, held captive by the tight, resisting band of muscle guarding the passageway.

Leaning forward, James dragged his tongue up from the root of Bram's rod to the deeply ridged underside of the head. Gaze never breaking from Bram's, James lowered his lips over the head and sucked it into his mouth. When Bram bucked and gasped, a thrill went through James, ending at his own leaking rod. James tongued at the underside of Bram's cock head and licked roughly with the flat of his tongue over the pulsing vein under the tip.

Unable to take the wide shaft down his throat, James relied on suction and swallowing to provide stimulation. Sucking hard, his used Bram's own trick of swishing and swirling saliva over the heated bulb.

When Bram's breathing began to falter in its rhythm and the sac resting on his palm contracted, James slid his fingertips farther up Bram's ass, scissoring them wide. He stroked and plunged in combination with the fierce sucking action, pressing his thumb into the skin under the sac, massaging the tissue surrounding Bram's prostate from the outside. His other hand wrapped around Bram's rod, milking, twisting and caressing its length in a measured rhythm.

James' heart was pounding and his breath came in shallow puffs through his nose. Untouched, his own cock ached, but the raw, animal look of need and desire on Bram's face made James forget about himself and renew his effects to please his lover. He sucked hard, taking the bloated tip to the back of his throat, swallowing around it, using his throat to caress the sensitive end through the protective covering.

James felt Bram's ass contract around his fingers and hands suddenly tangled in his hair. His lover bucked up, slamming into the roof of James' mouth. Bram's limbs spasmed as his orgasm hit and one hairy, stout leg shoved between James' thighs, the coarse, fine hairs skating roughly over James' cock, setting fire to his own blinding climax. James humped helplessly against Bram, all the while sucking and licking at the rod in his mouth. His eyes savored every contortion and lustful grimace that cross his lover's face, his own gaze mesmerized by Bram's commanding, intense, blue eyes.

With a guttural roar that shook the ceiling, the big man exploded into the sleeve with a force and volume that left his ejaculate dripping from under the condom's edges. Bram collapsed onto the cushion and lay there panting, still staring into James' face.

James slumped against the cum-covered leg between his thighs and let Bram's only slightly diminishing cock ease from his mouth.

Swollen and raw, his lips felt bloated and too large for his face. James closed his eyes, blocking out his partner's scrutiny, suddenly feeling exposed and unsure. He licked at his lips to soothe them, finding old cracks and new ones in the sensitive tissue.

Gasping at the suddenness of the move, James found himself gathered up into a rough embrace, held against a sweat-covered chest, his mouth plundered like a fallen city under Hun attack.

Bram's lips were demanding, but gentle, reminding James this wasn't a quick servicing of some stranger's needs. This was real, intimate, the start of a relationship already past the one-nightstand test.

James relaxed into the kiss, savoring the gentle way Bram explored the bruised contours of his mouth and lips.

When his partner released him, James leaned back on his heels and surveyed the damages, his throat too tight with emotion to comment.

Bram lifted his leg out from between James' and gazed down at the drying streaks of white on his calf. He held the leg up so James could see what he was talking about and smiled playfully down at his flustered lover. "Jamie, you dog, you!"

Chapter Three

The restaurant was busy, filled with Saturday night patrons. There was a spattering of families with children present but the majority of the diners were couples.

A short, swarthy man in a dark suit rushed toward them as Bram and James entered.

"Mr. Lord! How wonderful to see you. Mrs. Giovani and I were beginning to wonder if everything was well with you. It has been weeks since you were last here, weeks!"

Giovani shook Bram's hand, clasping the big man's wrist and pumping his arm hard.

Bram grinned down at his energetic, rotund host. "Been busy with a new contract, Vito. Living on fast food and candy bars."

Vito gasped. "We will not mention that to Mrs. Giovanni or neither of us will hear the end of it for months. I'm just glad to see you back." Vito smiled at James, standing silent at Bram's side. "A special occasion tonight, maybe?"

"Someone special." Bram rested his arm around James' shoulders and gave him the lopsided smile that never failed to touch a flame to James' libido. "Vito Giovanni meet James Justin. I wanted the best for him, so I brought him to 'Via Emilia' and Mrs. Giovanni's manicotti."

James shook the man's hand, surprised at the

powerful grip in the stubby fingers. "Hi. Pleased to met you, Mr. Giovanni."

"Vito, please! You are welcome in my humble restaurant anytime, Mr. Justin." Vito began walking toward the back of the restaurant, gesturing for the two men to follow him. "Come, come. I will have to get Mrs. Giovanni. She will want to know you have finally reappeared in one piece."

Bram leaned down and whispered conspiratorially in Vito's ear. "I actually had a dream about her sauce last night." He leaned a bit closer. "Sauce everywhere. Very messy, but satisfying."

Vito jumped back and roared with laughter. His eyes darted back and forth between Bram's unabashed grin and James' embarrassed blush. "We will not tell her that either. It will be our little secret, yes? Just between the men."

"I think that's wise, Vito. Save us both from some bodily harm." Bram smiled at James. He walked closer, and brushed hand over James' hip as they came to a halt in front of a u-shaped booth.

Without comment, Vito shoved the table to one side to create a bigger opening for Bram's large frame. Bram nudged James onto the curved bench seat, then slid in close beside him.

Vito snapped his fingers and a waiter appeared from nearby. He turned back to speak to Bram. "Your usual or would you like the menu for Mr. Justin?"

"You know what I like, Vito. Make my dream come true." Both men chuckled then Bram touched James' knee under the table. "How about you, Jamie?" Expectant, Vito and Bram both looked at James.

The warmth from Bram's hand seeped into his leg

and distracted him. James felt his heart rate quicken and he had to resist the urge to squirm. It was nice being in a place where the fact that he was on a date with another man wasn't an issue, but all the personal attention was unnerving.

Biting his lower lip, James considered his options. "Well, I like just about anything. Bram trusts you. What do you recommend, Vito?"

He had apparently hit upon the right answer. Vito beamed and clapped his hands. "I have just the thing, a special dish. You will think you have died and gone to heaven. Be patient."

Vito addressed the waiter. "A bottle of our best red. You know the one, Angelo." The young man scurried off and Vito excused himself. "Now I must see to things." He bowed and hurried away, leaving the two alone.

James leaned back into the deep leather of the booth, feeling its butter-smooth texture beneath him. Bram's hand still rested on his knee. It felt good, a gentle reminder he wasn't alone, possessive, but not too much. James liked this mountain of a man more and more with each passing hour.

Darting a quick look around the room to see who was watching them, James was relieved when all he got was a shy smile from a young woman who happened to look up from her plate at the same moment. He placed a hand over Bram's on his knee and felt his fingers instantly laced between Bram's longer ones.

"How do you like the place? I usually eat here a lot. The food is fabulous and atmosphere is homey. Vito and wife are terrific hosts. They always make me feel welcome, like one of the family." A passing waitress smiled and said a bright, "Good evening, Mr. Lord." Bram nodded and smiled at her.

"I think it's a great place." James watched the innocent exchange between Bram and the woman. Her glance lingered and James was surprised when a jolt of jealousy rippled through him. "Friendly." James frowned at the waitress. "Very friendly."

Incredulous, Bram squeezed James' hand. "Are you actually jealous?"

James blushed and tried not to duck his head. He half-heartedly tried to pull his hand away, but Bram refused to let go.

"That's such a compliment, Jamie." Leaning in closer, Bram lower his voice to just above a whisper. "I'll be sure to take the time to thank you properly later tonight. I may have to thank you several times."

Now James did squirm, his dress pants suddenly too tight and too warm for comfort. Bram winked at him and sat back as the waiter returned with the wine. Bram tasted it and nodded his approval before handing James a glass.

James took a sip and let the mellow tang of the grapes ease the dryness in his sore throat. Some of his unease melted away it. "It's nice here. Comfortable."

"Yeah, I think so." Bram leaned back, but kept hold of James' hand, bringing it with him as he settled more comfortably into the curve of the booth. He sipped at his wine and winked at another waitress as she greeted him.

He knew it was next to impossible for a man of Bram's size to go unnoticed, but James was amazed at how many people went out of their way to say hello. Bram was very well known and liked here. James' comfort level with the physically intimating and powerful man went up a few more notches.

James glanced down at their intertwined fingers and noticed a couple of Bram's knuckles had fresh abrasions on them. James brought their hands up from beneath the table and run his thumb just under one of the raw knuckles. "I've been so whacked out over the whole thing in the hall, I didn't even notice you were hurt. Christ!"

Guilt and shame over the incident with Williams came rushing down on him and bile rose to the back of his throat. "I'm sorry you had to get involved in that."

"I'm not." Bram frowned and took a deep breath before admitting, "I'm glad."

"What?" James' voice cracked on the word.

"I'm glad I was there. Glad I got the chance to stop that asshole from hurting you. Glad I was the one there for you afterwards." Bram smiled his lopsided grin and looked sheepish. "And yeah, I'll admit it. I wasn't lying when I told that creep I was possessive and protective of you." Bram's tanned face darkened a shade. "Maybe it's kind of early to say this, but I like how you make me feel when I'm with you."

Swallowing past the residual burn in his throat from earlier, James decided to plunge ahead and go through the emotional door Bram had left open. "How *do* you feel when you're with me?"

Leaning an elbow on the table, the big man hunched forward slightly and studied the wine in his glass. He swirled the liquid around and then took a sip, setting the glass back down on the table before answering.

James began to think he had misread the situation then Bram raised his head and smiled. "Needed. You make me feel needed. Appreciated. You let me have control, but you aren't dependent on me." Bram took another sip of wine then stared James in the eye, his voice suddenly very serious. "I don't want to be consumed by someone who wants me to orchestrate his entire life for him."

James let out the breath he had been holding and released his bottom lip from the tight hold his teeth had on it. "I don't like being told what to do outside of the bedroom. I can run my own life just fine."

"Then we're good, because I don't want to be your 'daddy'." The big man gripped James' hand tighter. "But honestly, it does give me a rush to see you all flustered and unsettled. Like in the alley last night, when you weren't sure what was happening. And earlier tonight, at your apartment, when you needed someone to anchor you down. I'm glad I was there."

"I'm glad, too, Bram. I don't want to think about what would have happened if you hadn't shown up." James stared off into the distance. He felt a cold knot of anxiety ball up in his stomach at idea of Williams being allowed to finish what he had implied he wanted to do.

"The apartment building is up for sale. I might have to move soon, anyway." James was suddenly very glad he had meet Bram. Pushing the incident aside, he smiled at Bram. "I don't think I thanked you for earlier."

The lopsided grin on Bram's lips turned into a gentle leer. "Oh, I don't know. You felt pretty grateful to me on the couch. My leg thought you were grateful, too."

A strangled snort of laughter escaped James and Bram joined him. James laughed until tears blurred his eyes. He had to wipe them away to see his food as their waiter placed a large tray of appetizers on the table and disappeared again.

"Okay, I guess we're even. We're both glad to be

with each other." James brushed away the last of the moisture from his eyes and looked over the food tray, trying to decide what to sample first.

"Yeah." Bram's tone was considering. "We go well together. I knew that last night. That's why I asked you out. I had a feeling about us being right together."

James popped a marinated shrimp into his mouth and sucked the sauce off it. He looked up to see Bram watching his mouth as he savored the shrimp. Feeling playful, he sucked slowly and ran the fleshy part of the shrimp over his lips once before he ate it.

Bram's breathing increased and his hand was back on James' leg, this time higher up. His large, hot palm slid around to James' inner thigh and his fingers boldly stroked the sensitive skin there, but didn't move any higher.

James tightened his buttocks and fought the urge to push his groin into the man's hand. He grabbed his wineglass and took a sip, while his brain scrambled for conversation to distract him from the tantalizing pressure under the table.

"Your business card said you work for 'Eclipse Construction'. They're a pretty impressive company. Even the architectural firm I'm at, 'Dunn & Piper', does a lot of business with 'Eclipse'. What do you do there?"

Bram relaxed into soft leather and tilted his upper body so that their shoulders touched, all the while tapping lightly on James' inner thigh with his fingertips. "Well. . ." Bram sighed.

Thinking Bram's hesitation as a sign he might be reluctant to admit he was a blue-collar worker after James had admitted at the apartment to being an architect, James hastened to let the big man know it didn't bother him.

"Hey, as long as you can support yourself," James smiled, "and can pay for dinner, I don't care what you do for a living." He popped another shrimp in his mouth, enjoying the way Bram's eyes immediately darted to look at his mouth while he chewed. "But I'm thinking, they wouldn't be so nice here if you couldn't pay the bill."

James delicately licked a tiny spot of cocktail sauce off from one fingertip. He felt a thrill race down his spine when Bram swallowed hard and licked his own dry lips.

His half-lidded gaze never strayed from James' face as Bram said, "I'm thinking of making someone pay right now, but it's not the bill." The long fingers on his leg tightened and James squirmed. Bram murmured seductively into his ear, "Bad boy tonight, is it? Maybe we need to rethink that punishment idea."

James' heart pounded in his chest and his mouth went dry with excitement, but remained silent. It would be interesting to see what direction Bram took this, whether he had been honest about his expectations from James.

"I think you'll have to owe me a kiss, a real kiss," Bram reached up and ran his thumb over James' lower lip, "for each time you cocktease. You're up to two right now."

Gaze locked on Bram's face, James dipped forward and captured the man's thumb in his mouth. He gave it the same treatment he had given the shrimp beforehand. He sucked on it, swirled his tongue over the callused pad then slowly pulled it from between his lips, letting his teeth rake over the surface on the way out.

"Would you like more wine, gentlemen? Dinner will be ready in just a few minutes." Not having heard the waiter approach, James jumped and pulled back from Bram.

The waiter glanced at the uneaten tray of appetizers. "Was there something unsatisfactory with the food, Mr. Lord? Would you like something else instead?"

Turning, Bram cleared his throat and shifted in his seat. He grabbed a canapé from the tray and prepared to stuff it into his mouth. "No, no, Angelo. This is fine. We just. . . got caught up in the moment." He put the delicacy into his mouth, chewed and swallowed, but his eyes were on James the whole time. "It's perfect. I've never had better."

His blush deepened and James dropped his gaze to the table. He picked up a breadstick and began tearing it into pieces.

"Ah." Angelo smiled at the blush creeping up James' cheeks and nodded. "Excellent, Mr. Lord." He poured more wine into their glasses, then left, a knowing smile on his twitching lips.

The two men looked at one another and burst out laughing, the sudden awkwardness dissolving away.

James was surprised the hand on his leg never left. Bram might have been caught flirting with another man, but he didn't appear to be embarrassed by it. The man's self-confidence was rock solid.

"You never answered me. What do you do at 'Eclipse'? I had this fantasy of you in jeans and a work shirt, all sweaty and covered in concrete dust, but now I'm having trouble seeing you that way."

"Why?"

"You're too self-confident, too take charge, to be a worker bee. I'm guessing management -- supervisor or project lead."

"Close." Bram smiled. "Owner."

"Owner?" James nearly choked on the piece of

salmon he had just swallowed. "Of 'Eclipse'?" He looked at Bram's self-depreciating smile. "Wow. I'm impressed."

Finishing off the last bit of wine in his glass, Bram shrugged. "Majority stockholder." He set the empty glass down and fingered with the edge of his napkin. "I have people who run the day-to-day nuts and bolts of it, but I stay involved in all the major contracts and have final say on what projects we take on. I work a site now and then, too."

"'Eclipse' does a fair amount of charity work. Is that your doing?" James was impressed. Bram's company was a leader in promoting fair housing standards.

"We do some low-bid contracts for public housing and a lot of high priced bids to help pay for them." Bram shrugged off the compliment again. "I try to keep a balance between what's good for public interest and what's good for the company."

"A man used to being in charge, but knows how to compromise. I like that." James bit at his lower lip, then soothed it with a lick. "It's . . . sexy." The hand on his leg inched higher, then stopped. James flexed his thigh muscles in an unspoken acknowledgment of the thrill the movement produced.

Bram refilled his wineglass and took a large sip. "It was my father's company and he liked a hands-on approach. He loved to create beautiful buildings. For him it was more art than construction. I took over when he passed away four years ago, right after my mom. I've tried to follow in his footsteps with the company."

A melancholy tone had settled into Bram's voice and James felt a need to erase the small frown from the big man's furrowed brow. "Well, he did a good job of creating beautiful art with you. He must have been a good man."

James let every ounce of attraction growing inside of him for this man show in his voice. Bram responded with a shy, appreciative smile that James cherished.

"Thank you, Jamie. And he was a good man." Bram took a steadying breath and stopped playing with his napkin. "I miss him." He sat up straighter and turned his full attention on James. "But the real guiding force in his life was my mom. She was petite, just a little thing really, quiet and intense. Kind of like you."

Bram reached over and brushed a strand of dark curl back from James' forehead, softly caressing the smooth skin with his thumb as he talked. "Same sapphire eyes, too. They both would have liked you. I'm sorry they aren't here to meet you."

James swallowed down the lump forming in his throat. The big man's sadness was almost palpable, making James' chest ache with the desire to share it and make it less of a burden for him to carry alone. "I would have liked to have met them. They sound great. They wouldn't have minded? That I'm a guy, I mean?"

"They wouldn't have chosen this lifestyle for me, if there had been a choice to be made, but they accepted it as something that just was. It was never an issue between us. Sure, they worried about me when I was younger, but as soon as I filled out, they figured I could handle any problems that cropped up."

Bram dropped his hand and lightly touched the red mark still visible on James' throat. "There haven't been any Williams in my life, I'm relieved to say. Not that there haven't been the odd coy remark or cutting comment when my back was turned, but not very many people come at me head on."

"I can understand that. I thought twice about just

talking to you."

Bram snorted and stretched his long legs under the table, hitting the bench seat on the other side, a good four feet away. "It's one of the detractions of being so big. I even had to find a hundred year old house with nine foot ceilings and seven foot doorways to live in so I didn't have to duck every time I went from room to room."

James' eyes lit up and he turned in the seat, careful not to dislodge the warm hand working its way up his lap. "I love old houses. They have some of the most outstanding architectural designs ever made."

His hands moved in the air in front of him, emphasizing and expressing his feelings better than his words could. "The Brant Hill District on the north side of town is wonderful. It's not as swank as the Talbot Oaks area, but there's one block of homes, from Cypress to Evergreen, that's amazing. I'd love to live in one of those homes."

James realized Bram had been staring at him as he talked non-stop, a delighted grin on his face. "Sorry, I get a little over-enthusiastic sometimes." He picked up his glass and took several sips from it, hoping to blame the heat in his face on the wine.

"No apology necessary. I like seeing some of that passion you keep bottle up inside come out." Bram slid his hand into James' crotch and lightly caressed the growing bulge he found. "I want to know what makes you passionate. What turns you on, what pushes your buttons."?

James began to pant. His hips pushed up of their own accord, seeking more, but Bram kept the pressure to a steady, light stroking.

The big man picked up a pastry from the tray with

his unoccupied hand and fed a cheese-filled morsel to his date. His thumb became covered in the creamy mixture. As he pulled back, James grabbed it. He swallowed, and licked the fallen droplets from Bram's thumb. He scoured the digit carefully with his tongue before taking it into his mouth and sucking it clean.

His own breathing uneven and rapid, Bram shifted so his broad back blocked their activities from view of the rest of the diners. "If this is what just talking about old houses does to you, I'll have to show you my place. It's full of interesting angles and miles of elaborate detailing."

James actually felt heat radiate off the big man in waves. He found it difficult to breathe.

"Especially my bedroom."

The pressure at his groin increased and James bucked up into Bram's hand. He took a couple of deep breaths through pursed lips to dispel the dizziness rippling through him.

"Lots of interesting . . . architectural features?" If he passed out right now, James wondered if he could blame it on the lack of air in the room.

"Uh-huh. My bed, for one is a great eighteenth century design. Only one I could find that I could fit in comfortably. You'll like it. It has plenty of room to stretch out. Lots of places to hold onto, sturdy enough to be tied to." The slow stroking kept rhythm with the soft fluctuations in Bram's voice.

James let out a soft, strangled moan. His eyes darted around to make sure they weren't making a public display of themselves, but all he could see was Bram. Every broad, muscled inch of the man filled James' sight. "Tied? Me or you?" James managed to pant out.

"Either. Both." Bram moved the last few inches

needed for them to make contact and whispered against James' lips before he gave him a chaste kiss. "Does it matter, baby?"

"I think the only thing that matters to me right now," James swallowed hard and wet his lips, "is how soon can we be there?"

A soft, but distinct clearing of a throat jarred both men. Bram stilled his hand, eased back and turned, making sure James was protected from any prying eyes.

The younger man knew he was flushed, and he could feel a fine sheen of sweat on his face. His breath still came in short, shallow gasps over chapped lips and his pants visibly tented. He wouldn't be standing up anytime soon. James made an effort to pull himself together, then peeked past Bram's shoulder to see who had interrupted them.

Vito stood at the table, a large bag of take out containers in his hands and a rakish grin on his face. He chuckled at James' soft moan of embarrassment and extended the bag to Bram. "Dinner for two, to go. I thought maybe this night would be better spent at home, yes?"

Bram laughed and accepted the bag, nodding. "I think you maybe right. Thank you, Vito. You're a very intuitive man." Fishing out his wallet, Bram tossed three fifties on the table.

Vito shrugged and tilted his head to indicate their waiter at a table several feet away from them. "Thank Angelo. He said you were distracting him too much for him to work."

James dropped his chin to his chest and mumbled a distressed, "Oh, God, Bram. He'll never let us eat here again."

Bram just laughed again and tapped the top of James' fallen head. "It's okay, Jamie. I think he'll forgive us as long as we leave quietly. Right, Vito?" Bram stood and motioned for James to join him.

Vito chuckled. "Not to worry. The biggest catastrophe of the evening will be if Mrs. Giovanni's cooking goes to waste. See to it that it doesn't, my friends, and all will be forgiven." He patted Bram's arm, tucked an unopened bottle of red wine under it and walked off, humming a love song James recognized from a popular Italian opera.

Picking up the loaded bag, Bram waited for James. James inched out of the booth then awkwardly gained his feet, trying to unobtrusively rearrange himself in his pants.

A sudden, painful pinch to one butt cheek made him jump, muttering a string of oaths under his breath. "What the hell did you do that for?" Shocked, James rubbed at his abused ass, trying to soothe away the deep ache.

"Just trying to help." Bram took James' arm with his free hand and began leading them to the exit.

"How did bruising my butt help anything?" Confused, but wanting to leave, James let the other man guide him out the door.

"Easy." Bram glanced down at the front of James' pants. "You can walk just fine now."

James suddenly realized the uncomfortable fullness was gone from his trousers. His erection had subsided the moment the pain had jarred through him. "Crafty bastard."

Bram grinned and let his voice take on the rough, sexy tone that had sparked James' interest from the beginning. "Don't worry, baby. I promise I'll make it up to you. I know a few uses for Mrs. Giovanni's sauce she probably hasn't tried yet."

Chapter Four

The drive to Bram's house took fifteen minutes, much of which James spent pressed against the passenger window, commenting on the structural style and elegance of the long established neighborhood.

They ended the drive on a short, circular driveway in front of a graceful, two-story, red brick home. Wrought iron rods, spirals, fence posts and grates adorned much of the building. There was even an elaborate weather vane topping the patina-colored, copper roof of an octagonal tower. The approaching twilight hid the rest of the home's period features.

Awed, James climbed out of the truck and followed Bram up the steps of the wide porch. He waited while Bram opened two heavy-duty locks on the entry door, and then preceded his host inside.

Once they passed through the marble-floored foyer, the adjoining rooms became massive, all boasting nine-foot, domed ceilings, stylized, ten-inch baseboards and oak hardwood floors. Ancient oriental rugs accented leather and dark oak furniture groupings and numerous original landscapes done in oils and watercolors hung on the walls.

They passed through one large, open room completely bare of furnishing. One wall was almost completely glass, a series of lead-paned French doors that opened out to a courtyard. James could see a small fountain and several stone benches outside. "What a great room! The natural light in here must be outstanding. Why don't you use it?"

"I was going to make it into an office, but it's just too big. It would be a waste." Bram looked around the mahogany-paneled room admiringly. "So now, I'm waiting for inspiration to hit me."

"Wow. It would be a terrific place to work. You should reconsider." James' gaze drank in every feature of the room, from its carved ceiling rails to its massive marble fireplace and built-in ceiling to floor bookcases.

"I'll think about it." Taking in James' delighted, awed reaction to the room, Bram's expression became thoughtful. "Something will come up."

Bram led James down a long hallway, pausing to hang up their coats on the way. They emerged in an updated, gleaming kitchen complete with granite-topped counters and a gourmet eight-burner stove.

"I don't know about you, Jamie, but I'm starving. What do you say we eat some of this before it gets too cold and then I'll give you a tour of the old place?" Bram set the bag of food on the center island and began to unpack their dinner.

James rubbed his hands together and sniffed the air. "I can't wait to see the place, and as much as I'd like to take up where we left off in the restaurant," he patted his stomach, "I'm running on empty here."

James joined him at the counter, taking a plate Bram offered, filled with Mrs. Giovanni's spicy-smelling, cheese-filled pasta sleeves covered in a thick layer of rich, meaty sauce.

"Those appetizers were great, but they only got me warmed up." James smirked and seductively licked a smear of sauce off his index finger.

Bram reached over and pulled the finger from James' mouth. He wrapped his hand around the enticing digit and shook it. "Put that thing away. At least until we've eaten."

Picking up his own plate and the bottle of wine, Bram pulled out a stool with his foot and kicked it toward James. "What time did you eat lunch?"

James slid onto the stool and started eating. "Skipped it. And since I don't eat breakfast," he chewed and swallowed a huge bite of manicotti, "this is the first decent food I've had since yesterday." He forked up another mouthful and chewed. "This is fantastic. Good thing Vito's open-minded. I could get addicted to this."

"We like the same foods. That's good." Smiling, Bram poured two glasses of wine and handed one to James.

The younger man accepted it, but took three more bites of pasta before sampling the vintage. "Sorry." James worked the solitary words in between bites. "Hungry."

"Don't apologize, eat." They ate in silence for several minutes, devouring the meal Vito had packed.

Bram hunched forward and wiped a speck of cheese from James' chin. "Make sure you're full. You'll need your strength for later."

Gaze locked on James' face, he licked the speck off his finger, and then pulled back and dug into his food. "We both will." Bram cleaned his plate in only a few hefty bites.

"That a promise?" James teased.

Bram's eyes became hooded and his voice dropped to that low, sultry tone that made James' stomach do somersaults. He hooked a boot under the rungs of James' stool and dragged his lover over to him in one swift yank, sliding his knees between the other man's slender thighs. He pulled James into an embrace and tilted the younger man's face up. His lips brushed against James' skin as he talked.

"A promise," he kissed the tip of James' nose, "and a threat. I believe," he placed another kiss on James' chin. "Someone has some punishment," he kissed one corner of James' mouth, "coming," then the other corner. "Don't you, baby?"

James groaned and closed his eyes, completely seduced by the gravel-rough sound of Bram's demanding whisper and the teasing, feathery touch of the man's lips. Food was forgotten.

James relaxed into Bram's tight embrace, arching his neck so the unmoving fingers laced through his hair had to tug harder to keep their grip. A thrill of anticipation rocketed down his limbs as the pressure from Bram's hand increased, and he was forced to angle his head back a few inches more.

"Oh yeah, baby, fight me. I'll remind you who's in charge." Bram yanked James' hips off the stool and onto his lap.

James' swelling cock rocked into the other man's stomach. He couldn't resist bucking against the hard ridge of solid muscles, and letting out a low grunt. "Fuck!"

Bram chuckled and clamped one long arm around James' bucking hips and pulled them in tight to still them. His meaty hand massaged and kneaded James' ass as he promised, "Soon, baby, soon. But when I say we fuck, and not before." He continued raining light, almost-caresses over James' mouth with his lips, occasionally snaking out the tip of his tongue to moisten a section of chapped skin.

Before long, James was panting and moaning,

unable to do more than endure the erotic pleasure of Bram's embrace and slow attentions. The tingling warmth centered in his groin grew, turning into a smoldering delight.

When the slow, steady pace remained unchanged, James began to resist the confines of the other man's restraining hold. He squirmed, gratified by the feeling of Bram's iron-hard erection digging greedily into his ass with each tiny shift of his hips. Hoping to encourage his lover to move faster, James contracted and relaxed the tight muscles of his buttocks, milking the curve of his ass over the growing bulge under him.

The results were instantaneous. Wiping food off the countertop with one sweeping motion of his arm, Bram lifted them both from the stool and slammed James down on his back on the counter.

"Uh!" James' breath was forced out of him. His head smacked down hard, but met a protective palm instead of granite.

Bram easily pinned James in place with his long body. He let go of James' hair long enough to grab both of his lover's wrists. He then pressed them onto the countertop, held imprisoned in one massive, sandpaper-rough hand.

"Oh, no, baby. Not yet." Bram settled his body between James' spread legs, covering the smaller man from hip to chest. He held himself up on one forearm to allow his partner just enough room to catch his breath. "I think it's time your punishment started."

Gathering his captive up, Bram slid one arm under James' shoulders and used his other hand to grip the younger man's smooth jaw line. He trailed hot, wet kisses along James' neck and up into his ear, then licked a path down James' profile from forehead to his Adam's apple. Nuzzling and sucking at the convulsively, bobbing knob, Bram raked his teeth over it, dragging a strangled moan from his lover.

A shiver racked through the body under his and Bram leaned up to whisper into James' ear. "That's my baby. Shake for me. Let me feel what I do to you. Share it with me, baby."

James shivered at the command. A sharp gasp pushed warm, oregano-scented air to swirl in and past his ear. Intent on pulling even more of a response from his unhurried partner, he arched and wiggled, then pulled one leg up to brace his heel on the countertop, bringing Bram's erection more firmly into contact with his own. His eager cock pulsed and strained against the added pressure.

"Jesus, fuck! Do me, just do me. Right here. Please!" James panted and strained against the hold on his wrists, desperate to touch and be touched.

Gripping the thin wrists tighter, Bram nipped James' lower lip and let his voice rumble up from deep inside his chest, sultry and hot. "Oh, I'll do you. I'll do you so hard and so deep, you'll swear to God you can taste me."

James' insides quivered and he felt the head of his cock leak and grow larger. One continuous tremor shook his entire body and his lover groaned into his mouth.

"Soon, baby, soon. Let's get your 'punishment' out of the way first." Bram captured James' mouth with his own and began ravishing it, biting the fullness of swollen lips. He sucked James' willing tongue into his own wet mouth to stroke it, then licked and bathed every millimeter of tender flesh on the inside of his mouth until

James' entire awareness was centered there.

When James was breathless and shaking, Bram released him, and turned his cheek to brush rough stubble over James' gasping mouth. "That's one kiss. I believe you owe me three."

Bram released James' wrists and pulled his partner's shirt up and off in one powerfully swift motion, tossing it to one side. He reached out and snagged the large plastic bag the food had been packed in off the edge of the counter. He pulled the bag through his hands, forming a long twisted strand of white.

James' gaze darted from the bag to Bram's face. "What's that for?" His voice trembled.

Staring down into James' wide eyes, Bram tied the bag around the smaller man's unresisting wrists, still obediently lying where he had left them. He stretched James' arms up to hook the tied wrists over one faucet handle of the sink in the long countertop.

"I want to use my hands." He yanked James' hips down so that his arms were fully extended. "And you're not allowed to." He nipped at James' lower lip and stared intently at him. "Don't. Move."

Bram grinned at the unintelligible grunt and whimper that answered his command. He raised himself up slowly, dragging his hands down James' body, stroking the lean frame as he stood up. "Good boy. I like that." He rubbed his erection against James' wide-open crotch and ran his hands up James' tense thighs.

"Come on, man. Do me!" James whimpered.

"Not yet, baby. You don't want it enough." Bram kissed James' twitching cock through his tenting pants. "You haven't begged yet."

His zipper was tugged down and his belt

unfastened. James felt hot fingers slide under the waistband of his boxers. His hips were lifted and within seconds, he was divested of every scrap of clothing, socks and shoes included.

Looking up through half-lidded eyes, James watched as the tanned and weathered man above him raked his hungry gaze over his tied and splayed body.

The big man's expression softened and his pale blue eyes suddenly mirrored more of the light in the room as moisture filled them. Gritty palms slid down the flesh of his thighs, brushed over his dripping cock, then crawled up his out-stretched, trembling torso, grating over the aching peaks of his nipples along the way. Bram's upper body followed his hands and his warmth settled over James again.

"God, you're so beautiful. Every fuckable inch of you, baby. Mine. Mine to have. Any way I want, any time I want."

Bram's whispered breath puffed across James' neck and gooseflesh broke out on the younger man's skin. The scent of wine, mixed with a sweaty musk that was all Bram, invaded his mind and a shudder of desire hit him so hard both men shook with the force of it.

Bram's palms caressed his face, forcing James to look up into his eyes. "Isn't that right, baby? Only mine. Say it for me." The last was spoken in a gravel-filled hiss of command that traveled straight to James' trapped cock.

He moaned and bucked up, panting his frustration into Bram's mouth as his engorged and neglected shaft was suddenly wrapped in a sandpaper-lined vise of heat and muscle. James gave a strangled scream as the rough, mauling grip worked him hard and fast. He tugged on his arms and felt the plastic dig into his skin, using the burn and pressure of the bonds to keep him grounded.

This was the second time this man had denied James the use of his hands during sex, denied him the pleasure of touching his partner, denied him an outlet for his need. Kept him on the edge, kept him wanting, kept him in a haze of passion and desire. James moaned and tugged harder on his arms, thrilled by the helplessness of his position.

But guttural, needy moans and pain/pleasure filled screams weren't enough for his lover.

"Say it for me, baby. Tell me to whom you belong. Say it. *Say it*!" Despite his demand, Bram made it impossible for James to respond, sealing their mouths tightly together in a devastating, consuming kiss that left them both gasping and flushed when he finally broke away.

Hand still milking his lover's cock mercilessly, Bram rolled his forehead against James' sweat covered brow and harshly whispered, "Say it, baby, say it. For me."

Swallowing hard to relieve the burning dryness in his throat, James gasped into the sweaty mass of honey-blond hair hanging down in his face. "Any time. Any way. Yours."

Gritting his teeth against the dual sensation of raw burning and fiery ecstasy Bram was creating at his abused groin, James closed his eyes and moaned, then begged. "Please!"

His eyes popped open when the rough, gritty sheath around his cock suddenly disappeared then turned into a satin lined fist and the strong smell of garlic filled the already spice-laden air. The abrupt change in sensation sent James reeling as his lover ruthlessly pumped, massaged and squeezed his newly slicked erection.

"Fuck-fuck-fuck-fuck-fuck!" His climax raced to the edge of near-eruption and hung there, sizzling down his nerve endings, but never setting off the major explosion.

"My baby needs more, doesn't he? I'll give you what you need. Come for me, baby, now." Bram tongued one of the healing brick-and-mortar abrasions on James' chest, then latched onto a taut, rosy nipple with his teeth, biting lightly and flicking the peak with his tongue.

James screamed, his climax spiking along with the warm burn of pain. He went rigid as fire swept through his body. Bram took no pity on him, milking his erupting cock until it was limp and James was shuddering and groaning with each new stroke.

"That's it. That's the way I like it, baby. Shake for me. Show me what I do to you. Show me." Bram sighed into James' neck, gathering the still shuddering man into his arms. Not waiting for James to recover even the power of speech, Bram unhooked the bag from the faucet handle and stood, pulling James' limp and unresisting body with him.

Still deeply buried in a euphoric, sex-induced stupor, James didn't object when his arms and chest were draped over Bram's shoulder. "Bram?"

"Don't worry, lover. I just thought it was about time we took this to a bed." Bram lifted James' slight weight, balancing the man on one shoulder, grabbed the open bottle of wine and left the room.

Startled, James grunted and grabbed at Bram's sides. "Hey, put me down!"

Laughing, Bram jogged up the stairs to the second story of the house. "Uh-huh. This is my caveman ritual. Get used to it, baby."

"Bastard." James grunted at each jostling step. "And you can kiss my ass, Caveman."

Bram brushed his hand over the taut, bare globes by his head, then planted a loud, wet kiss on the bruise spreading over the ass cheek nearest to him. He ignored James' indignant yelp.

"Anything you want, baby. Just ask."

Chapter Five

The bed was enormous by anyone's standards. The headboard was a good three feet higher than the mattress with a matching footboard. The carvings on them were gilded and hand worked by a skilled master craftsman of eighteenth century design. James was appreciating the work even before he stopped bouncing.

Bram had tossed him from one broad, hard shoulder onto the middle of the bed, and there, James lay, sprawled on his back, legs spread and tied wrists flung up on the pillows. The bedcovers had already been turned back and the crisp, cotton sheets were cool on his heated skin.

The room was decorated in various shades of blue and green. The massive bed, made-up in layers of these colorful hues, looked like a small ocean. James swayed and dipped on its surface as it rippled like tiny waves under his weight. He brought his hands down to his chest and prepared to push up on one elbow to view the rest of the room, but flopped back down as a large naked wall of sweaty muscle and chest hair rose up between his legs.

Bram crawled up James' body on his hands and knees. Slowly, like a panther appraising a long awaited, finally fallen prey. The look in his eyes reflected the same primal attitude, ravenous with desire and need.

James pressed back into the pillows and wet his lips, suddenly hungry again, this time for the taste of sweaty, male flesh. He rested his bound wrists on the curve of his ribcage, and presented his open palms to his captor.

"So, are you going to release me?"

The bulk of Bram's body settled over James. "Not just yet." The large man held his upper torso up from the other man's smaller, leaner frame by resting his weight on his brawny forearms.

Sweat glistened over the dips and swells of the well-defined, heavily muscled body. James longed to reach up and lick the moisture from the man's bronzed chest and taste the ripe tawny nipple buds beckoning to him just inches away.

But it seemed Bram had other plans. He pinned James' hands between them, his own rippling abdomen keeping the tied limbs in place. Propped up over his lover, he laced his fingers loosely through James' unruly curls and stroked the scalp beneath them with the tips, barely touching it. His own frame being longer than James' allowed Bram to be face to face with his lover and to nestle his now semi-erect rod against the soft strip of flesh under James' balls. Tucked between the heat of the tight sac and the warm crack of James' ass, he nudged the tip of his erection into the crease.

James' still limp and sated cock lurched at the intimate contact. His eyes flashed closed for a moment and he was treated to a burst of thrills when Bram undulated, grinding his hot groin down onto James. He opened his eyes to the sight of his lover staring down at him, a thoughtful, inquiring look on his tanned, handsome face.

Effecting a softer version of his usual lopsided grin, Bram caressed James' cheek with a thumb. "Before we take this any farther, I think we should get to know one another better, don't you?"

Chuckling, James returned the soft expression. "What? I think I've spent twelve out of the last twenty-four hours naked, having sex with you." He felt a burst of heat in his face, abashed and thrilled by the other man's desire to have more than sex from him. "Trust me, there isn't that much left to get to know."

A gasp escaped James as Bram flexed his lower torso and nudged the end of his cock tighter against James' ass. "I think there is." He continued stroking James' face with his thumb, tracing the line of the delicate cheekbone. "So far I know your name is James Justin. You're an architect with the prestigious firm of Dunn & Piper --."

"*Junior* architect," James interjected.

"Junior architect, sorry. Based on your job level, I'm guessing you're about twenty-seven --."

"Twenty-eight, thank you."

"I may have to gag you before we can get a conversation going." Bram brought his thumb up and tapped James on the tip of his nose to quiet him. "I know you live next to a sadistic creep, enjoy Mrs. Giovani's cooking as much as I do." He leered down at James. "Maybe more. I've never had her garlic butter sauce used to jerk me off."

Eyes wide, James' mouth fell open. "Is that what you used? Christ, she should bottle it as lube. It felt great, burny and slick and warm. From now on, just the smell of garlic will give me a boner. Jesus!"

The rumble of laughter from Bram's chest vibrated against James, the jerky ripples of muscle launching a new wave of need. James grunted and spread his legs further. Bram responded by burrowing deeper between his ass cheeks.

"And I know you like hot, brutal sex in dark alleyways with strangers from biker bars who make you beg." Bram thrust up forcing the blunt head of his cock to ride hard against the opening to James' body. "You don't seem like the biker bar type."

James grunted again and bent his knees, bringing his legs up on either side of Bram's sculptured hips. "Not." He panted a few breaths. "I was pissed about being passed over for the Becker project Friday. I wanted to go out and get laid and forget about the whole damn thing."

"Why the Atlantic? I know there are better pick-up joints for a guy in town."

A blush colored his face all the way to his hair and James lowered his gaze to study a point somewhere near Bram's chiseled chin. "I can count the number of lovers I've had since college, including one night stands, on one hand. I wanted to be with someone, but I guess not just anyone, you know?"

He gathered his courage and looked up at Bram. "So, I suppose, maybe, I picked a place where the odds of my finding an interested partner were on the low to never-going-to-happen side."

His eyes darted back and forth, taking in every aspect of Bram's face. His gaze trailed from the fine, laugh lines at the corners of Bram's pale blue eyes, the rough stubble beginning to erupt on the strong chin, to the endearing lopsided smile tugging at one side of the big man's mouth. James' bound hands clutched convulsively at Bram's stomach in the effort to hang on to the other man.

"I didn't expect," James swallowed hard and looked deep into his lover's eyes. "I didn't expect to find you. What was a guy like you doing there?"

"Remember the guy I was playing pool with? Ponytail, green head bandanna?" James nodded. "He's one of my crew, Mitch. Once a month I join him and a couple of the other guys from work to play pool there." He wiggled his eyebrows and leered. "I never expected to find a treasure like you there, either. It was my lucky night."

"Luckiest day of my life, so far." James' voice was soft and laced with a shy hesitation.

Staring into James' eyes, Bram slowly lowered his head and placed a chaste kiss on trembling lips. He kissed the tip of James' nose, each cheek, then gently nuzzled and mouthed each closed eye on his young lover's face. "I want you."

Reaching over to the bedside table, Bram pulled open the single drawer and rummaged through its contents one-handed. He produced a crinkled and creased sheet of paper and laid it on the tabletop before leaning down to plant a gentle kiss on James, this time on his ready lips.

"That says I'm clean. It's less than six months old and I've never had sex without protection, ever." Bram smoothed the stray curls back from James' forehead. "But I want to with you, Jamie. I don't want there to be any barriers between us, not even the thin wall of a condom."

Bram kissed him again and pried open James' mouth with his lips to dart his tongue inside the hot cavity. He coaxed James' tongue into his own mouth and sucked on it, stroking the silky underside until James moaned and writhed under him. He rested his forehead on James' brow.

"I want to be naked inside you, Jamie. I want to feel your tight, little ass grab a hold of my cock and milk it with its slick, hot walls." Bram pushed against James with his fully engorged shaft. James felt his ass grow warm and slippery from the fluid leaking out of the tip.

"I want to ram myself into you, reach the center of you. Pump my cum into you, flood you with it." Bram's lips rapidly worked their way around James' face to breathe heavy and hot into the delicate shell of his ear. He swirled and licked at the tender skin in between panted words of desire and urgent longing. "I want to know after I pull out, part of me is dripping into every crack and corner inside of you, coating you, with me . My cum, seeping into your body, into your soul, making you mine."

Bram panted heavily and rubbed his prickly cheek over James' jaw, feeling the muscles of his throat convulse. "I want to make you mine. Claim you. Let me claim you, Jamie. I want you to feel me inside of you. Every pulse of my cock, every spurt of juice, every hot drop of my load, just for you."

Rolling his head from side to side, James grunted out a jerky, lust-filled series of barely understandable syllables. "Dear God, yes, please! I'm good, too. Don't have a paper on me, but --." His words and thoughts were silenced by Bram's tongue thrusting down his throat.

James groaned, restless and frustrated, digging his fingertips into the smooth plains of flesh pressed against him, longing to touch more of this glorious, passionate lover.

Ending the kiss, Bram pulled back to sit up on his haunches. Taking hold of James' hips, he hauled them up his thighs and onto his lap in one swift, violent motion. He slipped his long arms under James' bent legs so the knees rested in the crooks of his elbows. His full cock strutted in the air, deep red and leaking, glorious and bold, its veins and ridges engorged and pulsing.

Gathering James closer, he grabbed both of their cocks in one massive, callused hand and pulled a few rough, fast strokes up the burning shafts.

James grunted at the sudden coarse caress and arched up into it, the raw, insistent grip heightening his need to touch. He reached out with his bound hands and was surprised when Bram yanked them forward and down, forcing them over their erections. His fingers were wrapped around Bram's stiffening thickness and his own shaft nestled between his restrained wrists. James clamped his forearms together to increase the friction on his own member and worked his two-handed fist up and down over Bram.

A deep, animal groan rumbled from the back of Bram's throat. He stared down at their joined bodies.

"Look at you. Look, baby, your bound hands, stroking my cock, working me over. It's so hot. Look at you. Look at us, baby. Do it." He ran his palms up James' sides and over his chest, leaning forward to pluck and roll his nipples into taut nubs of fire. "Look."

The change in position forced James to curl up tighter. He tore his gaze away from Bram's sweat-covered face and awed expression and did as Bram demanded.

The sight of his own stiff cock rubbing along the insides of his lashed wrists, rasping over the sharp edged wrinkles of the improvised restraint, made his head swim and his prick swell.

The feel of Bram's stout rod under his fingers was like satin over molten steel -- hot, heavy and growing. The flared, leaking head exploded through his fist like a mushroom growing in time-lapsed photography only to submerge and re-explode again and again. Creamy moisture spilled from its slit and coated James' hands, slicking the tight sheath of his fist. His thumb rubbed at the underside of the glans, massaging and teasing the rim.

James looked up to see Bram's face contorted into an anguished grimace of lustful, savage bliss. James had never seen anything so feral and erotic. He wanted to make this man explode with a white-hot pleasure so violent and so raw that he'd never look for anyone else but James to bed.

Increasing the speed of his strokes, James was startled to have his hands encased in a grip so powerful his fingers ached. He could only imagine the force being exerted on Bram's shaft. He was more amazed as his hands were pushed to the root and clamped down even harder.

"Jesus, baby! What you do to me!" Bram's panted and growled. "A little bondage and your sweet mouth and I'm popping my load before the evening gets underway. Holy Christ, baby, you're ruining me!"

The hot, harsh words washed over James like a tidal wave of lust and he shuddered. "Want you!"

Bram's primal growl grated into an anguished groan. "Fuck!" Panting like a racehorse, he grew rigid, eyes clenched tight and every muscle in his sculptured form tensed as he fought to delay and control his release.

Held motionless, James drank in the sight of the bronzed beast that had captured him and memorized every detail about the man. He watched a rivulet of sweat run down Bram's neck, then trickle over the man's bulging pecs to drip off the tip of his erect nipple, a drop at a time, and splash onto James' quivering belly. The effect was like being pelted with sparks from a raging fire.

James used Bram's crushing hold on his hands as a

counterpoint to pull against and surged up to lick the next drop of sweat from Bram's full tit. Latching onto the nub, he jabbed it with a stiff tongue and worried it with his teeth, pulling it taut, then releasing it as he slowly lowered himself back down to the bed.

His fevered gaze locked with Bram's near wild stare. He licked his lips to savor the lingering salty, musk taste of the man. "Take me. Pound my ass, caveman. Make me taste you like you promised. Claim me." Unused to verbalizing his desires in bed, James flushed, excited and embarrassed by his own words.

"I say when, baby. I say when." Reduced to a guttural rumble for speech, but in control of his body's responses once more, Bram released their shafts and plucked at a stray end of James' impromptu bonds. The plastic tie fell away, leaving deep red creases on the tender flesh.

Bram picked up both wrists and brought them to his lips one at a time, where he lavished the raw marks with wet, gentle laps from his tongue. He ended the bath by placing a kiss on the center of each palm, as he lowered James' arms to the bed. He leaned forward, slid his hands under the fullness of James' bum and chastely kissed his heavily panting partner.

"When." Bram's raw, hungry growl hissed into James' ear at the same time his backside was lifted and his cheeks separated. A blunt, slick rod of lava-hot steel drove through his tight opening and plunged deep into his channel.

"Fuck!" James arched his body and threw his head back onto the pillow; the intense burn of the sudden stretch painful, but eagerly embraced.

Expecting Bram to ram the length of his thick cock

to the root, he wrapped his legs around the man's waist, his hands braced on the man's broad, sweat-slicked shoulders. He shivered as the pleasant burn in his ass spread as his passage fluttered and spasmed around the intruder. Held motionless, James felt like Bram's heated palms were branding their imprint on his ass.

"Uh!" Bram groaned and pressed his head against James' flushed face. "Home again. God, I've been missing this." Another deep groan rumbled through his chest. "Missing you, baby."

He captured James' mouth and ravaged it, the kiss demanding and rough, relentless and overpowering, leaving no doubt in James' mind who was in control.

Bram began to thrust in long jabs, plunging deeper and deeper, impaling James' with a hammering motion that rocked the entire bed.

Wanting another taste of the beefy man plundering him, James swiped his tongue over a dusky nipple. Bram grabbed him by the hair with one hand and pressed his mouth to the crinkled bud. "Oh yeah, baby, suck it, suck me. Uh, ugh, oh yeah. That's it."

Patiently dragging his cock out of James' flared and clenching hole, Bram slowed down his thrusts, letting the tight muscle caress the entire length until the underside of the engorged, bulbous head emerged and spread the sensitive ring of nerve endings to their limits. He released his hold on James' head to better brace himself. When he reentered the hot, moist tunnel, he added a thumb, stretching and massaging the inner ring with its callused surface. His still fattening rod drove in and battered the clinging, velvety walls. James shuddered and bucked, clenching his ass.

Grunting between gasps, Bram clamped his fingers

on James' hip and worked his own rod in and out of his lover like a piston. "That's my baby. Shake for me. Take me in. Feel me driving my cock right into the heart of you." He wrapped one hand around James' long neglected shaft, ruthlessly stroking the leaking head with the abrasive pad of his thumb. "I'm going to cum for you, baby. Fill you up with my juice. Cum with me. Let me see you spurt."

"Christ!" James was reduced to babbled grunts as the flood of sensations in his ass clouded his mind. Burning pain, sizzling heat and a rapidly building rush of electrical passion fused together and peaked. "Fuck-fuck-fuck-fuck!"

The inarticulate sounds rose to a shriek and then died, frozen on James' lips as his throat, his cock and his ass all spasmed. Creamy threads of viscous fluid erupted from him to coat his abdomen. The overwhelming intensity left him weak, befuddled and pliant, only conscious now of the throbbing fullness stretching and pounding into his raw ass.

His dwindling shaft remained trapped in the tight sleeve of Bram's hand until the big man released him and grabbed both of James' thighs. He yanked James deeper onto his lap, embedding his pulsing cock as far into his dazed lover as physically possible, and froze.

James groaned and convulsed around the unyielding shaft, feeling the hot flood of juices being blasted up his ass to bath places no one else had ever reached. His cocked twitched and shivered at the thought and he instinctively palmed it to soothe the sudden ache.

The sight of Bram caught in the peak of orgasm was like a holy experience for James. Like some bronzed god from ancient mythology, the man loomed massive and proud, sculptured body held rigid as stone, rugged face a mask of feral ecstasy, enraptured and euphoric in the release of his ravenous lust. It was that moment when James fell in love.

As the paralyzing fever of blinding climax tapered off, Bram gasped in a needed breath and opened his eyes to his own vision of sated lust. His gaze raked down James' sweaty, cum-splattered body. He licked his lips and softly growled, low and deep in his chest.

Despite the fact that the man had just fucked him senseless, James felt the heat rise on his skin and knew he was blushing. Their lovemaking was dirty and brutal and raw, filled with lustful passion and animal need. It was perfect.

Gasping, James hissed and clenched the muscles of his hard-ridden ass as Bram eased him off the still half-hard shaft.

"Whoa, there, baby. Nice and easy." Bram guided James' ass back down on the mattress and gently lowered his bent legs, briefly rubbing at the calf and thigh muscles.

Dropping to his side, Bram flopped over James' leg and flattened himself along side of his exhausted lover.

"Jesus, Jamie. What you do to me, baby." Groaning, he spread a hand over James' hip, then pulled him into a deep, gentle kiss that threatened to reawaken both their lagging libidos.

James lost himself in the moment. Bram's warm hands kneaded his sweat-chilled flesh and caressed the base of his spine. A feeling of contentment washed through him, making him feel boneless and happy. Every cell in his body seemed to thrum with satisfaction, even the ones that ached and burned.

He melted into the embrace. Bram took command

so naturally. He took care of James' deepest needs, created a whole new group of hidden desires, and satisfied each and every on of them. Remembering how his bound hands had looked wrapped around Bram's proud, reddened shaft, James shivered.

"Umm. I like that." Bram ran a heated palm up his arm chasing away the goosebumps. "Cold, baby?" He reached down and pulled the covers up from the bottom of the bed. Bram tucked the sheet and light comforter around James, then drew him close to his side and draped a heavy arm over him. Playfully smirking he added, "Or just happy to see me?"

Snorting, James lightly punched the furnace-like flesh next to him and rubbed his nose into Bram's chest hairs. The warm musk of their combined scents permeated the air. James ran his hand down his own abdomen, tracing the path of drying secretions. "Want to shower? Most of you is inside of me, but all of me is all over us."

The other man chuckled and pulled James nearer. "Uh-uh. I like the smell." He nuzzled his nose into the space between them and inhaled deeply. "It's us, all mixed together, connected." His expression turned somber and he gazed into James' eyes. "Mated." He placed another lingering kiss on James' pliant mouth.

"Mated?" James swallowed past the growing tightness in his throat. He studied the contours of Bram's chest rather than let the other man see the hope he knew was in his eyes. "That sounds . . . serious."

"I am serious. You're special, Jamie. I know to trust my gut instincts, and they're telling me this is right. I want you. And not just in my bed now and then." One rough, callused hand cupped James' chin and tilted his head so their eyes could meet. "I want you, Jamie, by my side, at my table, in my bed, as a very big part of my life."

"Jesus, Bram."

A burst of heat shot through James so intense it made him ache. It spread warmth all the way to his fingertips and toes. Not only did this man know how to make love to him until his head spun and his body screamed, he knew what to say. James wanted to take a chance on a relationship with Bram. A real relationship, not just a few nights of mutual satisfaction followed by stilted self-conscious conversation.

"What do you say?" Bram's thumb traced the curve of James' chin, over and over, petting and calming him. "Give me a chance to show you how loyal and domestic I can be."

Uncertain, James dropped his gaze and snorted. "Domestic? The caveman? Primal and ravenous maybe, but definitely not domestic." He clenched his ass and intensified the deep, burning, glorious ache left behind by his dynamic and passionate lover.

"Wait until you get to know me better," Bram purred from deep in his chest. "I'm as domestic as an old house cat."

James laughed and ran an appreciative hand over one of his partner's thick, muscled biceps. "More like a saber tooth tiger. I feel mauled." Reveling in the solid strength of his partner, he slung an arm over Bram's waist and leaned into him. "Very good, but definitely mauled."

"Only good?" Bram squeezed James' butt cheek hard enough to make the other man yelp. "I must be losing my touch." His voice turned sultry, rich with promise. "I'll have to try harder next time."

"You do and I won't be able to walk." James shimmied his groin against Bram's thigh. "Sitting is going to be a challenge as it is."

"That a problem, baby?" Bram roughly massaged James' tender backside. The dull, throbbing discomfort shot bolts of pain/pleasure through James.

"No." James' voice was ragged and breathy. "It's actually kind of nice." He bit at his lower lip, and then released it to blurt out, "I love it." Locking gazes with Bram, James confessed, "I could get addicted to you."

Bram rolled over, pinning James partially under his weight. He ghosted his fingertips down his lover's sweaty flank. "Think it's a passing addiction, or could I hope for a lifelong condition?"

James shifted his gaze for a moment, but Bram wouldn't let him turn away. "Afraid it might get to be terminal," James whispered.

Bram touched his forehead to James' furrowed brow. "Nothing to be afraid of, Jamie. I told you, I'm as domestic as they come. Commitment doesn't scare me. It makes me stronger. My parents and sister taught me that. I want you." He gently kissed one fluttering eyelid, "Want to make you happy," and then the other. "Want to love you."

"Love." James trembled under the weight of the word. "You're talking major step, Bram. We barely know one another."

"And I want to spend a whole lot of time changing that, Jamie, a whole lot of time, decades, if we're lucky. A few minutes ago when we left the shower cap in the wrapper -- nothing separated us. That's how I'd like to see us - open, honest and laid bare, so there's no question about how we feel about each other, for us or anybody else."

Panic pressed down on James. He felt his pulse

hammer through his veins. His stomach churned into a tight ball of ice. "You mean, you, like want to meet my family?"

"Hell, yes! Family, co-workers, friends, the world, want to meet them all. I don't hide my sexuality, Jamie. I didn't think you did either."

James dropped his gaze, speaking softly. "I don't make an issue of it." He concentrated on the intense heat building up wherever their bodies were in contact, memorizing the feeling for future fantasies.

"Me either. I don't flaunt it anymore than Mitch harps on the fact he loves the ladies. Any ladies, some are so ugly, I'm not even sure they are female. He's not very discriminating."

The playful comment managed to pull a brief smile from James.

Bram rewarded him with a quick kiss on the corner of his mouth. "But I'm not ashamed of who I love, anymore than Mitch is. It may mean I have to put up with a few crude comments and the occasional crass remark from some ignorant S.O.B., but I won't live a secretive, miserable life to spare someone else's self-righteous morals."

James snorted inelegantly. "A person would have to be insane to harass you."

Bram closed his eyes for a moment. His voice took on a distant, flat quality. "You'd be surprised just how many nuts are out there, Jamie. People who want to hurt you, for no other reason than you exist and it has nothing to do with who you're sleeping with."

"Williams would never have bothered you." James was surprised at the amount of bitterness in his voice.

Hovering over his lover, Bram settled his weight

on James and pressed him into the soft mattress. "Let's forget about that asshole for now." He slid his arms around James then swiftly rolled onto his back, dragging the other man up onto his body. "He's interfering with an outstanding post-fuck cuddle."

James squirmed, rearranging himself into a more comfortable position on his new bed of warm, supple flesh. "Didn't know cavemen were so romantic."

Twisting his head down, Bram craned his neck to see James' expression. "A bad thing?"

Rubbing his hands over Bram's solid ribcage, James shook his head and smiled. "Uh-uh, caveman. Good thing."

James rested his head on the broad plain of Bram's well-developed chest. He buried his nose in the soft, v-shaped mat of hair under his cheek to breathe in the delicious musk scent that was all Bram's own. Sweat and leather, now mixed with the heady scent of their combined sexual gratification and release. The air was rich with it. One whiff made the muscles of James' ass flutter and his cock twitch with appreciation. Even the scratchy peel of their dried juices on his skin sent a tingle of delight through him.

How did something that usually would have him insisting on an immediate shower become a turn on? Was it just exhaustion or the fact the scent and feel was now associated with the man who had caused the spectacular creation of the mess in the first place?

James decided it didn't matter really. He loved it, craved it, didn't ever want to move from the spot where he was -- safe, warm and very well loved -- wrapped in the arms of this brutally forceful, romantic mountain of a man who satisfied desires James had only fantasized about, not all of them sexual. He was amazed at how his life had been turned around by one small, chance meeting. He was amazed and grateful.

James felt heavy tendrils of sleep intruding into his thoughts. His exhausted, sore body welcomed the invitation to temporary oblivion and he relaxed more fully into Bram's embrace.

"Jamie?" He felt Bram kiss the top of his head.

"Uh-huh?"

"Sleepy?" A large, warm hand gently ruffled his dark curls.

"Uh-huh."

"Comfortable?" Bram's voice was seductively low and honey smooth.

"Oh, yeah."

"Happy, baby?" Another rough-skinned, heavy hand kneaded his back.

"Hmmm."

Bram snorted a low, throaty chuckle. "Sex must short circuit the speech center of your brain." His voice became playful, as well as sultry. "Overwhelmed by my amazing sexual wiles?"

"Mmmm."

"Completely under my power?" Bram studied what he could see of James' face that lay pressed against his chest.

"Umm." The sound was barely an audible grunt, followed closely by a light snore.

Bram continued the soothing petting motion down James' back in silence for several moments, then whispered, "Love me?"

Draped over the broad chest, James' body rose and fell along with Bram's deep sigh. "More with every silly-ass, annoying question you ask me, Caveman. Now shut up, and let's get some sleep. Being fucked senseless wears a guy out."

Without opening his eyes, James rolled his head to one side and nipped nearest strip of smooth-muscled skin his lips and teeth could find.

Startled, Bram jerked at the sharp sting, then laughed so hard he rocked the entire bed, needing to bear hug James to keep him in place. He planted a quick kiss on the younger man's head as he firmly patted James' ass.

"That's my baby. Sweet-assed, little tiger with sharp teeth." He gave James a quick squeeze, rested his chin against the top of his lover's head and relaxed onto the pillows. "Love you too, Jamie."

Chapter Six

Morning brought James a whole array of new aches and sore muscles, but not a single one he regretted. He awoke face down on a firm, unfamiliar mattress, naked, sore and horny. James drew in a deep breath to clear his mind and the rich, heady scent of recent sex filled his senses. His half-hard cock instantly responded, expanding and twitching in anticipation. Eyes still shut; he rolled over onto his back to give it more room to grow. As he turned, his elbow connected with a large, warm mass that immediately engulfed him as a stout limb wound around his body.

"Morning, baby." Firm lips kissed his temple and a fever-hot hand slid down his abdomen to wrap around his stiffening, delighted rod. "I see you're no worse for wear."

Bram. That one word brought a grin to James' face. He arched up into the heavy caress and opened his eyes. His lover lay on his side, propped up on one massive arm, hand supporting his sandy-haired head. The other hand was busy making James' morning memorable.

"Uh. Jesus, Bram. Nice wake-up call. Uh. God." James hissed and closed his eyes again, narrowing his focus down to the one part of his body wide-awake and functioning.

"Too sore, baby?" Bram mumbled into James' mouth then quickly kissed him.

"Uh! Ugh. Not enough to ask you to stop." Ignoring the usual date courtesy of limiting exposure to morning breath, James gasped and pulled Bram back down for another longer, more satisfying kiss.

Their dueling tongues ignited the big man's lust. James actually felt the surge of power ripple through the hard body. A burst of gratification erupted in his chest at discovering one of his new lover's sure-fire hot buttons -- the simple act of kissing fueled the beast in Bram.

James' sensitive cock was nearly raw from their savage couplings, but one swirl of the sandpaper, rough thumb over the eager tip and the burn of discomfort morphed into the burn of desire.

Just as James crossed over the line from pain to pleasure, Bram's hand disappeared. "UH! What the hell!" His startled complaint was cut short, the tight fist returned, this time bringing with it a satiny, wet coating of cool gel.

"Holy shit! Fuck!" James jerked his knees up and spread his legs, bucking up to glide in and out of Bram's skilled grip. One hand grabbed Bram's stroking arm and the other darted down between his legs to finger his own sac.

"Christ, baby, seeing you like this, all wet and slick and hard, it's too much." Bram's words were throaty and paced between rough pants. "You're beautiful. Fucking delicious, too." He paused every few words to kiss or lick a patch of skin on James' face, neck or chest, even his armpit. "Too delicious for a quick hand job."

Lost in the delirious sensation of having his cock worked over by a silk-slick sheath of hot muscle, James didn't register the change in activity on the bed until he was being flipped in the air, powerful hands clamped to his hips. Blankets disappeared and he landed face down on the mattress, his lower half bent over a mound of pillows, his small, firm ass raised high in the air.

Despite his rising libido, he didn't think his ass could take another brutal pounding so soon. James looked over his shoulder and tried to twist around to face Bram, who was kneeling between his spread legs.

"I don't know . . .. I mean, we've been going at it pretty hard . . .." James' voice trailed off in a stammer. He had purposely fanned the flames of the big man's desire, and now he was trying to throw cold water on it. He doubted Bram would be impressed by a cock tease.

Two solid, insistent hands jerked him back down on the pillows and a tendril of fear shot through him. James' heart skipped a beat. A rough-skinned hand soothed up his spine, then skated back down to rub his clenched butt cheeks.

"Easy, baby, easy. I know what you need." The hand kneading his ass was urgent and rough, Bram's voice tense. "This tight little hole of yours is just aching to be stroked again."

James stiffened and forced his groin deeper into the pillows as his cheeks were spread apart, his body held in place with a heavy hand on his low back. Cool air drifted over the exposed pucker of muscle and the ring fluttered. Every spasm burned and James gasped at the odd mix of cool air and hot pain at his entrance.

Bram groaned. "Look at that. Your ass already knows who it belongs to, baby. It's all swollen and dark red." He made a deep, guttural sound somewhere between a chuckle and growl. "Looks just like a cherry." Bram leaned forward and licked a few inches up James' spine.

"Bram, I-I don't think . . . shit!" James shivered as the moisture cooled on his hot skin, then shuddered when the tongue bath was repeated again, once up each flank.

The groan from the man behind James was like a big cat's rumble, silky and primal. "Yeah, that's it. Shake your sweet ass for me, baby. Fucking tremble under my hands."

A thumb rubbed lazy circles over his swollen, exposed pucker. James flinched and bucked, not sure whether to pull away or impale himself on the teasing digit.

"Uh, Christ, baby. Gotta have your cherry red ass."

The other man's urgent desire was heavy in his tone. Despite his hesitation to be fucked, James' cock hardened and twitched against the confining pillows in response.

Hands slid under James and he was pinned to the bed as long arms hooked around his thighs. The firm globes of his backside were spread open. Bram's rough-silky voice murmured, "I wouldn't hurt you, baby. Trust me. It's all about trust between us from here on out." Then Bram plowed in.

"Bram!" Burying a strangled cry in the mattress, James grabbed a handful of the sheet under him and held on, gritting his teeth at the sudden shock.

Curved and stiff, Bram's tongue speared through the red, abused opening to his lover's overworked ass, tormenting the tight ring of nerve-filled muscle. Bram attacked James' ass like his first meal after a week long fast. He licked, bit and sucked every millimeter of the opening until it relaxed and spread, still fluttering and clinging around the impaling force of experienced muscle.

The same talented tongue Bram used to kiss James into a shuddering heap of wanton flesh ravaged his now gaping asshole like a devil-possessed animal. James felt his orgasm already building. He wormed one hand under his body and reached for his neglected cock. Instead, his wrist was clamped in a beefy hold, as Bram intercepted him. He tried to tug loose, but he was held tight.

"Uh-huh. No touching, baby. Going to make you cum just like this. Pinned down," Bram squeezed James' trapped hand tighter, "ass held high and spread wide," he roughly kissed first one quivering globe then the other, "so I can eat your sweet, cherry-puckered ass until you scream."

His throbbing cock swelled to its limits and James moaned helplessly into the mattress. Warm air puffed against his saliva-wet hole making it clench at the sudden chill, sending a shudder up his spine. The shivers had the added bonus of rubbing his frustrated cock over the wrinkled folds of the pillow.

Desperate to touch something, James grabbed at the wrist under his restrained hand. He was surprised when the hold on his wrist was released and his fingers were interlaced with Bram's strong, thick digits. A shudder of pleasure washed through him when his hand was gently squeezed then held.

Bram stabbed at the sensitized opening, rolling his tongue and forcing small spurts of spit up James' ass. He rubbed the tip of his tongue over the slick, clinging passage as far as he could reach again and again. Using the broad width of the muscle to rasp over the swollen entrance, he sucked and nibbled the raw, tender tissue outside until James writhed and bucked under the assault.

James' struggle increased as his orgasm built to a painful level. He gripped Bram's hand harder and savored the returned pressure almost as much as the sizzling climax that traveled down his spine and exploded up from the root of his aching cock, making his sore ass burn and clench. The burning pain scorched through his body and tore a cry from his dry throat. "Ugh! Bram!"

Panting into the sheets, James melted against the support of the mattress and the pile of wet pillows. A lingering kiss was pressed to the base of his spine. Bram slid up to lay beside him. James turned his head and opened his eyes to see the other man staring at him, a soft, loving expression on Bram's handsome face. He slipped a hand down the front of Bram's body to automatically return the favor, but found a limp and sticky shaft nestled against a stout thigh. Bram shrugged and offered his lopsided grin.

"What you do to me, Jamie." There was wonder in his voice as Bram raised their still entwined hands and squeezed. "What you do to me." This time it was said in contented acceptance.

He brushed a lock of sweaty hair from James' forehead, gaze darting from the younger man's deep blue eyes to his full lips and high cheekbones, seemingly memorizing every feature. Then Bram smiled and rapped a knuckle on the top of James' head.

"Ow!"

"Come on, sleepyhead. Go get a shower while I get breakfast started." Bram rolled over and sprang from the bed like a cat.

James admired the way the big man's entire body rippled with controlled power and grace. From his muscled neck to his bulging biceps, triceps, tapered hips, firm ass and thick shaft, the overall view was outstanding.

"What about you? Want to join me?" James was actually a little concerned what the answer would be. He ached all over. It was a delicious ache, but painful nonetheless.

"Next time." Bram winked at him. "I think we could both use a little 'down' time." He pointed at his inactive cock. "Besides, I've been up for over an hour." He began dressing, sliding into a pair of jeans and a button front shirt over a black T-shirt. "Showered, cleaned up the mess we left in the kitchen and brought your clothes upstairs." He gestured to the open doorway to the left of the bed. "I folded them and put them in the bathroom for you. I found a disposable razor and a comb in my travel kit you can use. I put them on the sink with a new toothbrush."

Sitting up on the edge of the huge bed, James blinked at the clock on the bedside stand. It was 7:32 am, on a Sunday. "Wow. It's early."

Chuckling, Bram sat down next to James and pulled on socks and a pair of well-worn, brown cowboy boots. "I usually like to be at a work site by 6 am, most weeks six out of seven days. I have to make the most of my days off, so I get up early then too. If I need more sleep, I go to bed earlier."

He leaned over and gave a dazed James a quick kiss on the lips. "But with you here now, that probably won't mean I'll be getting more rest. Just more bed time." He stood up, pulling James to stand with him, then gently pushed the other man towards the bathroom. "Get going. I have plans for us. Unfortunately, you have to be dressed to do them." He lightly groped James' bare ass as the younger man moved away. "Just hang the toothbrush up in the holder when you're done."

Stumbling to the bathroom doorway, James paused and looked over his shoulder to watch the other man stride out of the room. Bram was power, grace, intelligence, looks and possessed a skill as a lover James was sure would eventually cause him to spontaneously combust during climax one day. And the man wanted him.

Turning on the shower, James decided the next time he was down on his knees he was going to say a prayer of thanks -- just before he sucked the big man's soul out through his dick and swallowed it whole, so nobody else could have it.

***

When James came out of the bathroom, the bed had been changed, and the room straightened. The only reminder of their activities was the lingering scent of their release.

Taking in a deep breath, James was starting to see the attraction Bram had for it. His libido took notice immediately. Out of a new sense of self-preservation, James hurried from the room. He was already walking a bit cautiously.

Arriving at the kitchen door unnoticed, James watched his lover work. Bram had shed his outer shirt and stood facing the stove, broad back and firm butt nicely defined by his clothing. Every movement he made was done with grace and control. He flipped pancakes, turned sausages, buttered toast and poured coffee like an experienced short-order cook. Bram turned around to place two brimming plates of food on the now sparkling countertop they had made out on the evening before.

In form-fitting jeans, a clinging T-shirt, and sinuous muscles in obvious quantities, the small mountain of a man was the poster boy for anybody's wet dreams. It was just his opinion, but James thought the ruffled, red plaid apron tied around his waist was especially endearing. He couldn't help but react.

At the sound of laughter, Bram froze then lowered the plates to the counter and turned to face his heckler. His lips twitched as he fought to maintain a stern expression. "Find something amusing, do we?" He began to move slowly toward the other man.

His newly acquired sense of self-preservation kicked in again and James smothered his laughter and edged away, moving to the other side of the large island counter.

Bram continued to stalk his prey, moving like a wild cat on the hunt, matching each evasive action his victim made.

"No, no, really." Edging around the island, James bit his lower lip and widened his eyes, the picture of innocence. "I think it's . . ." His hands gestured vaguely at the apron as he searched for a word that wouldn't get him killed and failed. "It's . . . adorable."

His stalker's eyes narrowed and James knew his time on this earth was dwindling. Laughing, he dodged to the right then cut to the left, only to be seized from over the top of the island.

Bram yanked him over the smooth granite surface and into his arms, narrowly missing their breakfast. Spinning his laughing prey around, he pulled James into a sitting position on the edge of the countertop and settled himself between his captive's legs. Lacing his fingers together behind James' back, Bram pulled him close, pinning the other man's arms between them.

A top edge of a plaid ruffle ended up tucked under the big man's jaw in the playful struggle. He had to nudge it down with his chin to speak with any dignity.

"Adorable?" He growled like a cat, too.

"Did I say adorable?" James' whole body shook with the effort to remain solemn. "I meant . . . red's your color."

Bram's eyes narrowed again and the stern expression on his face cracked a bit as one corner of his mouth twitched. "Yeah?"

Biting his lip, James nodded. "Uh huh. But I'd ditch the plaid if I were you." He nodded again at the raised eyebrow Bram gave him. "Makes you look chubby."

"Why you little ungrateful shit." Bram's finger's unlaced so he could heave James up and over his shoulder, ignoring his partner's yelps of protest and stuttered giggles. "It's not my fault your mother forgot to feed your scrawny ass." He swatted James' butt once and dropped him onto a stool. Bram held on tight, fingers massaging the body under his hands. "Delightful as that ass is."

Shaking with laughter, James took a moment to get his balance after being upside down. He clung to Bram's arms still wrapped around him.

Bram pressed his chest to James' back and nuzzled his ear, then murmured into it. "That's the way I like to feel my baby shake for me. Because you're happy." He quickly kissed James' cheek and pulled away, squeezing James' shoulder as he moved to his seat. "Breakfast is getting cold, let's eat."

Laughter tapered off to muted chuckles and James nodded. "No arguments from me. I'm famished. Burning off a lot of extra calories lately, for some reason." James wiggled his eyebrows at Bram and dug into his food.

Grinning, Bram winked and smothered his pancakes in syrup. "Just think of me as your own personal

Bowflex from now on."

Taken by surprised, James inhaled his coffee. Bram clapped him on the back, unsettling the smaller man from his stool.

Lying on the floor at Bram's feet, James continued coughing, but begged, "Stop helping, before you collapse one of my lungs!"

Bram lifted James up off the floor and helped him regain his seat. "Sorry. I have to get used to holding back a little with you." Bram released his hold, but James grabbed his arm to stop him from moving away.

Catching Bram's puzzled gaze, James looked intently up at his new lover and whispered, "Don't you dare." He stayed locked on Bram's face until he saw the puzzlement dissolve into understanding and acceptance.

"Okay, I won't." Bram's voice grew soft. "But I'm warning you right now, Jamie, my sense of commitment tends to be even stronger than my body." His expression was loving, but firm. "And I think it's only fair I get the same in return. Can you handle that?"

James' stomach tightened as a small wave of nausea washed through him then dissipated under the other man's gentle gaze. "For you, I'm willing to try."

Bram was silent. He studied James' hopeful, but uncertain expression. One hand came up to rest on James' shoulder and he left a small tremor run through the man. He slowly slid his hand up to gently trace the outline of James' cheekbone with a callused thumb. "Then that's all I can ask for. Right now." He dropped his hand and returned to his food. "Let's finish up. The day's wasting away."

Nodding, mainly because a lump of fear blocked his vocal cords, James picked at the remainder of his meal, eating just enough to keep Bram from commenting on his absent appetite. How could he be so afraid of something he wanted so much?

Afterwards, James helped clear the table and he washed the dishes. Bram dried and put them away since he knew where things belonged.

When the last dish was put away, Bram hung up his apron on a hook by the stove. James snickered, but one warning look from the big guy had him biting both lips to keep a straight face.

"You really are domestic. With a capital 'D'."

"Told you so." Bram wiped down the countertop with the dishrag then hung it up to dry by the sink.

"I can't believe you managed to change the bed *and* make breakfast while I was in the shower." James followed Bram out of the room and down the hallway to the front foyer.

"Didn't want to have to take the time to do it later." Bram turned and winked at James. "Might be in a hurry to use the bed."

Blushing, James took the coat Bram handed him. "I like a man who plans ahead." He slipped the light tan jacket over his wrinkled pale blue dress shirt and navy trousers from last night. "Where are we going?"

"Not far." Bram reassured him. "You'll see."

"Okay." James zipped up his coat and glanced up the front staircase leading to the bedroom. "And speaking of showering, that's an amazing bathroom you have upstairs. Did you design it yourself?"

"Yep. It was originally a nursery off the master bedroom. This place has a lot of rooms." Bram pulled on a brown leather blazer. "The walk-in closet, on the other side of the bedroom, was a sitting room. That's one of the best parts of living here -- lots of space."

"God, these old houses are great. I'd love to live in one someday." James gazed around the massive, formal entrance he was standing in, awe in his eyes and his voice. "The architectural features and craftsmanship are so unique in each one. I have a lot of respect for the men who made them."

Watching James' expression, Bram smiled and looked around the room again with a light of new appreciation on his face. "Glad you feel that way, because you, Mr. Junior Architect of 'Dunn and Piper', and I are going for a walk."

He turned and opened the front door, gesturing for James to join him. "This whole neighborhood is full of houses just like this one. And most of the owners have tried to keep their improvements as true to the original design as possible. I've even worked on a couple."

He slung his arm around James' shoulders and pulled him close. "I want to show them to you. Kind of introduce you to the neighborhood. You'll love it." He guided them both out the door and down the broad stone steps to the sidewalk.

***

By the time they had circled the entire block, stopping to talk to whomever was outside, Bram had introduced James seven times. And each and every introduction made it clear James was an architect, an expert in the period their houses were built in, and he was Bram's boyfriend.

The first time, James was taken by surprise. By the last introduction, he was faintly more comfortable with the term and Bram's openness. He knew it was the big man's natural charm and easy self-assuredness people were responding to. James found just being with the man made him more self-confident.

The classic architecture and fine, old-world workmanship sparked a familiar excitement in James, energizing him. He forgot his initial shyness, talking structure and design, and pointing out how the personal tastes of the individual craftsman's building it were worked into every detail of the home. The homeowners loved him.

Bram quietly watched, pride and delight in his lover's child-like enthusiasm and impressive knowledge easily read in his pale blue eyes.

The neighbors accepted James as easily as they accepted the large, charismatic man hovering possessively at his side. James received invitations to come back from everyone.

Walking side by side as they turned towards home, Bram nudged James with his elbow. "So what do you think? Nice neighborhood, huh?"

Stepping closer as they walked, James felt Bram's hand brush against his hip. "This is a terrific street. And I don't mean just the houses. The people are nice, too."

They came to the front sidewalk leading to Bram's place. They stopped outside the wrought iron gate to the walk and James gestured at the house. "You've got a great place and it's *in* a great place." He let his hand brush over Bram's knuckles.

"So, you like it?"

"I like it." James slowly reached out and slipped his fingers into Bram's eager hand. "A lot."

"Yeah? Attracted to the architecture then?"

"Oh yeah. But I like the fact that you're here, best of all." He leaned into the big man's space. "Your basic structure and unique build is still the most impressive thing I've seen all day."

Bram tightened his fingers and pulled James up against his chest. "Maybe I should take you on a tour. Let you get to know some of the structural details better."

Tilting his head back so he could see Bram's face, James smiled at the lopsided grin he found there. "I do like the 'hands on' approach with a project."

"Oh, there'll be plenty of 'hands on'." Bram ran his hands around James' hips and rested them on his backside. "Mostly my hands on you, but you never know."

James felt a stirring in the other man's groin as it pressed against his abdomen. He returned the interest by shifting his own groin to brush Bram's thigh. "I'm interested in finding out." James licked his lips, pleased when Bram's gaze dropped to follow the movement.

"Then I think we should take this indoors." He released his hold and threw an arm around James' shoulders, guiding him toward the front door. "We can combine the tour of my structure with a tour of the shower you were so taken with earlier."

Chuckling, James said, "But I don't need a shower."

Bram unlocked the door and pulled James over the threshold. "I can fix that."

Chapter Seven

Once the front door closed, Bram slammed him up against a wall and pulled him into a kiss that raised gooseflesh over James' entire body. Long arms wrapped around his lean frame and two strong hands gripped the curve of his ass, hiking him up the wall until his feet no longer touched the floor, kneading and groping to their heart's content. All he could do was dig his fingers into the fabric of Bram's shirt, hook his legs around the braced, solid thighs pressing between his legs, and hang on.

His lips were coaxed open by a warm, insistent tongue. James slowly stroked it with his own, sucking gently, and milking the muscle like an offered tit. A deep groan from Bram forewarned a change. The hands on his ass disappeared and James was suddenly pinned to the wall by the weight of Bram's chest pressing on his and one thick thigh forced up under his crotch.

James didn't need to open his eyes to know what was happening. The fabric under his hands was torn and flung away. The roughness of the act made his nipples harden and James moaned into the mouth still ravishing and invading his. His own shirt was peeled from his body and questing, sure fingers found and opened his pants.

Bram made one, quick heavy grope at the rising cock tucked inside James' pants then he regained his hold on the firm ass balanced on his leg and pulled his lover off the wall. He made it halfway up the stairs before James' hand managed to squeeze between them and down the front of his own jeans. The big man faltered then leaned forward settling them both on the stairs.

Bram broke the kiss and leaned back, panting and sweating, flushed. He rubbed both thumbs over James' swollen and puffy lips. James sucked one into his mouth. The flush creeping up Bram's neck shot up to his hairline and passion filled his eyes.

"Christ, you get me going like nobody else can, baby." He reached down and pulled James' shoes and socks off, tossing them over his shoulder, unconcerned where they landed. He dipped down and lavished several broad swipes of his tongue over James' chest, working his own jeans open in the process.

James ran his hands down Bram's chiseled torso and followed the trail of fine hairs down past the sensitive navel to dip into the open v of the zipper. The moment he touched burning flesh, Bram yanked his hands up and threw them up on his own shoulders.

"Not yet, baby. No touching. I want to take this one nice and slow." Bram suckled one crinkled nub on James' chest then released it. "Want to let it build, until every square inch of me is screaming to have you." He suckled then bit the other peaked tit.

"Fuck you!" James moaned then panted, bucking against Bram's leg rubbing seductively over his groin.

"Maybe." Bram grinned, watching a flush spread like wildfire up James' chest, igniting a bonfire of lust in the younger man's dark, expressive eyes. Bram's breath caught and shifted his grip again. "Hold on, baby. We're halfway there."

Resisting the urge to yelp, James wrapped himself around Bram and hung on. The big man rose to his feet, barely hindered by James' additional weight, sealed his mouth back over James in a blistering, possessive kiss and covered the distance to the bedroom in no time.

Once through the door, Bram lowered James to stand, but held them together in an increasingly demanding kiss. His hands continued down James' body, sliding his remaining clothing off to the floor. Bram lifted James up again and kicked the discarded clothes aside. Pulling James' legs up around his waist, Bram walked to the bed, dropped his jeans and sat down, settling his lover in his naked lap while he toed his boots, socks and jeans off.

Wanting to help undress his impressively built lover, James tried to pull out of the kiss, but each time Bram just growled and increased his attentions, pressing them closer together. James learned to breathe around a second tongue in his throat. His cock was fully engorged and leaking, aching for some of the same lavish attention his mouth was receiving. He reached down to stroke it, but his hands were immediately pinned behind him.

Bram flopped on the bed onto his back bringing James along with him. He rolled them over pinning James' arms under them and ending the kiss with a tug to James' bruised lower lip.

"I can see this is going to be another time when I have to teach you to listen, baby." He ducked his head and bit the cords of James' neck at his shoulder, sucking and marking the tender flesh.

"Goddamn caveman." James shivered and moaned, pulling away then pushing up into the sharp sting. "Oh, yeah, oh god, yeah."

Bram ran his hand over James' sweat-slicked skin tracing the path of the small shudders still echoing through the smaller man. As the last of the tremors died away, the big man growled and lifted them both off the bed. He swept their naked bodies into the bathroom, banging the door open with his shoulder then kicking it shut with his heel. He walked directly into the shower stall.

The shower was a huge walk-in, built into one entire end of the spacious room. It sported a deep trough, several drains, and four-foot walls on either side of the opening. The walls had double, adjustable showerheads on adjustable arms at various heights all around the large, tiled cubicle.

There were little cubby nooks at staggered heights embedded all over the walls, each equipped with a thick metal rod handgrip. Two of the higher rods had an old-fashioned soap on a rope laced around each of them. James had wondered what these were for during his earlier shower.

Bram pressed James up against the cold tile wall between the soaps. James gasped and his cock wilted a little at the shock, gooseflesh broke out again and he shivered. His hands clenched hard on Bram's shoulders, leaving finger shaped marks in the heated skin.

Bram moaned and dropped his head into the crook of James' neck, burying his face and inhaling. "God, I love the way you smell, baby." He licked his way up James' neck and jaw pulling James' face down by a firm grip in his hair. He murmured over James' lips, sucking gently on one swollen lip then the other as he talked. "Love the way you taste. Way you feel." He ran his hands up and down James' thighs wrapped around his waist then under the firm ass, where he roughly fondled the tight globes, brushing lightly over James' overly sensitive opening.

James shuddered and sighed at the teasing touch

from the hot, thick fingertips.

"Oh, yeah, baby. Love the way you tremble best of all." He held James in place with his body and raised one of James' arms up the wall over their heads. Grabbing one end of the soap rope, he pulled until the soap slid up to the grab bar then looped the rope securely around James' wrist twice. Staring James in the eye, he did the same to the man's other wrist with the second soap rope.

James stared back at Bram, startled, but willing to play along. He let his eyes say so for him. Bram seemed to instinctively know just how much James could deal with in this bit of rough play they had going between them. James wasn't going to stop him now. Even if he wanted to, his cock wasn't going to let him. It stood straighter and taller and more eager with each turn of the ropes. By the time Bram was done, James was panting and straining against the bonds. He rested his head back against the cool tiles and looked up at his taller lover, thrilled and a little frightened by the wild, possessive look in Bram's chiseled face and lust-filled gaze.

Taking a savage, deep-throated kiss from his breathless lover, Bram slowly released his hold. He let James' legs slide to the floor, and he stepped back, memorizing every inch of James' lean, flushed body. His gaze lingered over several places, taking extra time at James' swollen, parted lips, the deep purple mark on his arched neck, the thin trail of dark hair that led to his hollowed stomach and slightly curved, beckoning cock.

Bram licked his lips. "Going to get to know all about you, baby, *all* about you." He turned on the water, adjusted the temperature and began directing showerheads to spray over James.

"Going to make you so hot." Bram moved forward

again and tugged on the ropes. He licked playfully over James' lips, but kept their bodies from touching. "I want to hear you scream my name again."

James' voice was husky with need. "I can do that now. Just touch me." His dark eyes pleaded, the pupils dilated with desire. He whispered back into Bram's still hovering mouth. "Please."

Still keeping his physical distance, Bram's lips brushed over James' mouth with each word he spoke. "I'm going to, baby. Eventually, when you realize you can't live without me touching you."

Warm water pulsed onto James' chest and sides. A second showerhead sprayed a teasing, fine mist over his groin. James spread his legs to let the trickling water run in rivulets down the crease of his groin and over his aching balls.

The air grew thick and heavy, clouds of moisture filling the room with a ghostly haze. A fine sheen of sweat popped out on his face and James squirmed against the rapidly warming tiles at his back. A slight tug on his arms reminded him of his helpless position and his cock sprung forward, growing and straining with each pull on the ropes.

A metal basket attached to the wall by the faucet handles was filled with an assortment of brushes, sponges and bottles of gel. Bram selected a soft, scratchy net ball and a bottle of green tinted gel. Standing directly in front of James, he soaped up the sponge and worked the ball into a foamy lather, his intense eyes never looking away from James' face.

Starting at James' out-stretched arms, Bram worked his way down the front of his lover's body, stroking and caressing every square inch of skin above the other man's waist. He concentrated on sensitive armpits and flank areas, lavishing the lean muscles and straining tendons with multiple passes of the soft, silky foam. James' nipples received extra attention, the sponge pressed more firmly against the erect nubs, swiping again and again until James was moaning and writhing.

Out of habit, James sucked in his lower lip and bit it to keep silent.

"Come on, baby, talk to me. Tell me what you need. I know you want to." Bram encouraged in a sultry whisper.

James moaned, closed his eyes and shook his head.

"Talk to me, baby." He lightened his strokes until James was arching off the wall to maintain contact. "Talk to me. Now, baby."

All contact disappeared and James' eyes popped open. He strained against his bonds and whimpered. "More." He was rewarded with the return of the silky caress. "Yeah, yeah, like that. Ugh! Again. Harder. Please." Voice hoarse with need, James arched his back seeking more.

Bram went to his knees, trailing the sponge down one side of James then the other, following the curve of thighs down to the arch of each instep. He pointedly avoided James' bobbing erection, narrowly skimming down the crease of his groin and back up. The pulsing, swollen shaft swayed, leaking a milky fluid that was washed away in the warm mist of the shower's spray.

James looked down to see Bram's broad shoulders and water darkened hair. Small streams ran down the tanned flesh, diverging and merging as they followed the dips and valleys of the well-defined muscles and sinewy limbs. The deeply tanned skin shone like bronzed metal.

From this angle James could see Bram's own nipples were peaked and rosy, the flesh full and erect. James longed to be able to lick and suckle them. He moaned then whimpered, the impact of his loss of freedom becoming even more torturous as desire and lust magnified at the sight of his magnificent lover on his knees before him.

Words of longing caught in his throat, making him grunt out unintelligible sounds of wanton need.

The distressed groan brought Bram up from his knees. He looked at James' flushed face and quivering body for only a moment before acting.

Sighing in relief, James nearly cried out when one of his wrists was released, fingers automatically reaching for Bram's water-slick chest. His relief was short lived.

"Fuck! Bram! What?" The last was more of a desperate whine than a question.

"No touching, baby. Warned you once already." Bram bit the lobe of his ear and the sharp tingle of pain made James shiver despite the heat of the room.

He was spun around face to the wall and his wrist looped up into the rope with his other one.

Bram nudged James' legs apart with his foot and ran the slippery sponge down James' spine, letting the satiny smooth suds gather at the small of his back where they ran into the crack of his ass. Bram followed the sudsy track and rubbed the gritty surface of the net sponge over James' raw, fluttering asshole.

"Tell me." Bram scoured over the opening, adding just enough pressure to make the contact erotic not teasing.

James shoved his ass higher in the air and gasped. "Oh, god, yeah, more please."

Bram played with increasing pressure, varying the length and area he stroked, never giving James enough to reach a peak of excitement, but not allowing him to fall complacent either. He sponged lower over sensitive inner thighs, then forward to nudge the tight sac hanging unprotected and inviting between James' spread, trembling legs.

James wrapped his fingers around the cords binding his hands until his knuckles turned white, concentrating on every sensation his skin was transmitting to his fevered brain. He forced out the sounds of the water and the soft murmur of Bram's breathing, trying to intensify the little thrills of excitement traveling up his spine from his ass. His cock thumped against the tile wall and he squirmed to feel the ridges of the grout where it met smooth tile in an effort to provide more stimulation to his shaft.

Just as he found a rhythm and pace that fed his approaching climax, he was suddenly spun around and knocked against the wall. Looking up into Bram's face, James' breathing hitched at the scorching glare the man gave him.

"Uh-uh. That's cheating." Bram held the sponge directly above James' erection and squeezed a dollop of suds onto the reddened tip, letting the silky foam drizzle down the length of the heated rod.

James hissed and clenched his eyes, torn between shaking off the maddening tickle and savoring every slow oozing bubble on his sensitive skin. The sensation faded away as the fine spray of water pelted him and James realized that was all he felt. Opening his eyes he was greeted by a sight that took his already labored breath away.

Three feet away from him stood his tall, broad shoulder, bronzed god of a lover, naked, muscles sharply defined in the bright light of the shower spotlights, skin slick and shiny with water and sweat. Just out of reach, but definitely not out of sight.

James slowly raked his gaze up Bram's body until he found his lover's handsome, chiseled face. Bram's expression of primal hunger mirrored his own thwarted cravings. But Bram could do something about them. James squirmed at the thought of the imposing, restrained physical power waiting to be unleashed in his lover. Bound, all James had was his voice. His lover knew it was difficult for James to verbalize during sex -- knew it and was using it to his advantage.

"So tell me, like what you see, baby?" Bram's voice was like a cat's purr, rumbled and silky rough. "Maybe you need to see more before you can decide?"

Bram flexed and stretched under the now pulsing spray of water, never lowering his sultry gaze from James' face.

James' attention darted from one impressive muscle group to the next. Droplets of water, like tiny prisms refracted in the shower spotlights, rained down on the smooth, sun-darkened skin, highlighting every curve, bulge and smooth plane. James wanted to follow their glistening trail with his tongue. He moaned and strained against the rope.

Biting his lower lip, James watched as Bram struck a provocative pose in front of him. He jutted his tapered hips forward, forcing his fully engorged cock higher, letting the natural pulsing movement of the straining shaft mesmerize and taunt James.

"See anything you like yet, baby? Tell me what you

like. Tell what you want me to do to you." Bram ran his hands down the creases of his groin to his balls, fondling and displaying himself, but never touching his heavy cock. "Tell me."

James bit his lip harder and tightened his grip on the rope binding his hands, but any words that came to mind sounded inadequate. He settled for a strangled grunt. "Ugh!"

"Not good enough, baby. You have to tell me."

Adding more gel to the sponge, Bram soaped and caress his own body, swiping deliberately over the glistening flesh, purposely avoiding his groin. After the front of his body had been bathed, he leisurely gelled his hand and brought it to his erection. Stroking the proud shaft in one meaty hand, he palmed and kneaded his chest with the other, working his nipples taut. His gaze never once left James.

James felt his temperature rise and his breathing grow more labored with each pass Bram made over his shaft. He watched his lover's hand glide up and down, circling the huge bulbous head with his thumb and fingering the weighty sac nestled between his firm, stout thighs. Bram moaned and brought James' attention back to his handsome face, now baring a grimace of lustful need.

"God, baby. I'd love to feel your sweet lips wrapped around my cock. Love to have your hot, little tongue lapping at me," Bram stroked himself in time to the rhythm of his words, "licking out the slit," circling the head with his fingers, massaging the leaking fluid from the tip into his skin, "eating up my juice."

Stepping closer, Bram pinched his nipples and rolled the peaks hard between his fingers. "All for you, baby. It's all yours. Would you like that?" He dropped his gaze to James' straining, leaking cock and licked his lips provocatively, whispering in a throaty purr thick with desire. "Or would you like me to take your sweet, juicy rod down my throat? Huh, baby? Would like me to swallow you whole? Suck the cum right out of you until your balls ache?"

Panting, James arched off the wall, trying to narrow down the distance separating them. The spray from the showerheads had turned from soothing to torturous, each new burst of water was like being pelted with sharp pins and the comforting warmth of the water was now a stifling heat. He could feel his pulse pounding in the base of his cock, the shaft so hard and aching, he thought the skin might split. James suddenly felt lonely and isolated. He needed to feel Bram's tender-rough touch to soothe him and take away the unbearable ache blossoming in his chest.

"Suck me!" James gasped, tears running down his face. "Please, Bram, suck me. Suck me dry."

Instantly closing the gap between them, Bram grabbed James' face and gently kissed away the tears on his cheeks, adding a light kiss to each eyelid before sealing his mouth to James' lips. Bram kissed him, deep and hard, pressing his heated body along James slender frame, enveloping the smaller man completely in his embrace. "Anything you want, baby. All you need to do is ask."

"Suck me. Just suck me, now." James returned the kiss with fevered enthusiasm, biting and licking over Bram's lips, cheeks and jaw. As Bram drew away, James surged forward and sucked on the man's strong chin, mimicking the act he was requesting.

Running his hands down James' straining, writhing body, Bram fell to his knees, nudging James' legs farther apart as he dropped. Without preamble or warning he took the slender, hard shaft into his mouth and began to slowly swallow it, inch by inch, taking care not to give too much stimulation at once to draw out the moment.

James bucked and cried out, pumping his hips into the blissful heat of Bram's talented mouth, pulling the rope confining his wrists to its limit. A gel slicked finger brushed over his hole then wormed its way into his ass, massaging and coating the tender insides. It was all the added push James needed. Spurting and bucking into the tight suction of Bram's throat, James convulsed and screamed. "Bram! Jesus, fuck!"

James felt like his balls were being sucked up through his cock. He was dizzy and disoriented from the heat and the rocketing swiftness of his orgasm. The moment he started to soften, he was released, a hot hand replacing the hot mouth, skillfully fondling his half-hard cock to respond.

Opening his eyes, James found himself facing the shower wall. Bram plastered his body to James' back and his throaty gravel voice, strained with pent up lust panted in his ear. "God, you're so beautiful when you cum, baby, so beautiful. All stretched out and helpless, all hard and ready for me, begging for me, coming for me. You are so beautiful, my beautiful baby."

Rough hands kneaded James' nipples and fondled his shaft back to fullness. When both tits were hot and swollen, Bram moved his hand down to massage and rubbed over James' backside, roughly spreading and gripping the firm globes, letting a rivulet of hot water run over the slicked, puckered opening.

"Want me to fuck you, baby? Is that what you need?" Bram stroked James' cock. "Want my cock buried deep inside of your tight little ass? Would that make you happy, baby?" He jacked James harder, his gel-slicked hand moving smoothly over the thickening rod, fingers rimming the tip and tracing the pattern of pulsing veins.

"Yes, goddamn it." James grunted and pushed into the harsh grip, seeking more friction. "Fuck me. Just fucking fuck me."

Bram kissed his lover's shoulder then bit the curve of his neck, adding teeth marks to the purple bruise already branding James as his. "Anything for you, baby, anything."

With one powerful surge of lustful energy, Bram breached James' opening and plowed into the hilt, driving the smaller man off the floor and up the wall. Bram held James in place with an arm around his waist and one under a bent leg, gripping the thigh hard enough to leave bruises.

Resting his forehead on the wall beside James, Bram whispered in his lover's ear while he pounded mercilessly into James' ass. "Feels so sweet, so tight, so right. My baby feels so good."

Wanting to regain some control in their coupling, James reached up and grabbed hold of the metal bar the rope was tied to above his head. Pulling his body up, he shoved back against the iron rod sliding in and out of his opening, squeezing and twisting his ass with each brutal impact. "Harder! Fuck me harder! Split me in two, caveman. Give it to me." James shuddered and trembled, impaled again and again on the thick, long rod so far his stomach muscles fluttered. His orgasm ripped through him unexpectedly and James screamed out his surprise. "Christ! Bram!"

The ripples of climax transmitted down James'

rigid body to his still thrusting lover. Bram gripped both of the slim hips hard, heaving and pounding with a raw, primal energy, drinking in every quivering tremor. "Jesus god, baby, that's it, shake for me, shake for me. Show me how much you love me."

The word love made James gasp, lost in the haze of orgasm and the all-encompassing fullness slamming into him. A burst of pain mixed with a lightning quick blast of bright pleasure streaked up his spine as Bram shifted slightly and hammered over his prostate. James tightened his raw muscles to repeat the sensation, feeling the shaft inside of him grow and pulse.

"So close, baby. Almost there." Bram grunted and strained, his voice a tight whipcord of control. "Gonna fill you up, make you mine. Show you no one can do you better than I can." He arched his back and shoved deeper, gasping his words in hoarse, strangled breaths. "You're mine, baby. All. Fucking. Mine."

James felt the blast of cum flood his ass, amazed at the heat and volume of the load. Impaled motionless on Bram's spurting rod, he gasped and bucked as a new sizzle of excitement burnt along his nerve endings. His over-sensitized body responded to the throbbing iron rod still bathing his inner walls with liquid heat, clenching. The broad cock head pulsed against his prostate and stretched his fluttering inner muscles to their limits. One last rapid, unexpected, brutal plunge in and out of his abused hole and James' cock spasmed and spurted for the third time, leaving a small smear of pale juice on the wall.

Dizzy from the heat and weak from the exertions, James looked over his shoulder to tell Bram he was going to pass out, but croaked out the words that had been running around and around in his head all day instead.

"God, I love you, you bastard."

Warm arms wrapped around him and James melted into the embrace then slipped into the rapidly gathering darkness.

***

He woke to the sensual feeling of warm, rough-skinned hands massaging and caressing his body. James slowly took in the fact a massive heat source was plastered along the length of his body and his head was pillowed on a hard-muscled arm covered in smooth, supple flesh. James' muddled brain had no problem identifying his comforter, the big man's scent and touch was imprinted on the most instinctive, primal parts of his body and brain.

The mattress dipped and James was carefully turned from his side to his back. He sluggishly opened his eyes to see Bram's concerned expression melt into a relieved, but self-satisfied smile. He watched as Bram struggled to keep the smug part to a minimum, a slight twist in the corner of his mouth giving him away. Curling into his lover's possessive embrace, James settled comfortably against the larger man and sighed contently.

"You're a bastard." He burrowed his head into the crook of Bram's neck to nip at the soft flesh under the big man's jaw. "I thought the caveman routine was just a joke."

"I told you to get used to it." Running both hands down the length of James' back, Bram lightly massaged his lover's lean, wiry frame, mapping muscle and bone with his fingertips. "Not that I'm complaining, but I didn't realize I would be carrying your sweet little butt so often."

A large hand strayed lower and rubbed appreciatively over one of James' cheeks.

James jerked his head up to give the big man a narrowed-eyed glared. "And who, exactly, was responsible for my *needing* to be carried?"

With a self-satisfied gleam in his eyes and a wide, unrepentant grin on his lips, Bram smugly said, "Me. And don't you forget, baby." He pulled James up closer to his chest.

Snorting indignantly, James kissed the end of Bram's chin, locking gazes with his lover. "I'm not likely to forget the first time I was fucked unconscious, Caveman."

"Good." Bram pulled James completely up onto his chest and framed his lover's face with his large, work-rough hands. James paid more attention when Bram's voice turned husky and his tone serious. "I don't want you to forget who's the only one who can take you that far -- love you so hard, so much, so well, you see stars and blackout." His fingertips gently caressed James' temples. "And I mean *love you*, not just make love to you." His gaze never wavered. "I love you, Jamie."

Bram's blue eyes were warm, filled with more longing and desire, more naked love then James had ever seen directed at him in his entire lifetime. Even his parents hadn't loved him this much. Not before they found out he was gay, and certainly not since.

"Bram, I think . . . I . . .." Something in the middle of his chest hitched and tore, the sudden ache and accompanying dizziness making James' gasp. He involuntarily clenched his hands, gripping the hard-muscled flesh of Bram's shoulder and upper arm tightly enough to leave marks. He was amazed Bram's expression never changed, the man barely noticing the bruising pressure, his concentration locked on James' face and reactions.

James had started falling in love with the outgoing, straight shooting, mountain of a man in the alley behind the biker bar. He was completely taken with him by the time they had taken their walk around Bram's neighborhood. After what happened in the shower there was no point in fighting it. He was in love and there was no stopping it.

"I'm pretty sure I said it out loud in the shower, but I'll say it again, just in case you missed it." James forced his hands to relax, palms rubbing soothingly over the reddened flesh under their hold. "I love you, too, Bram."

Eyes slightly brighter, one corner of Bram's mouth twitched as he tried to hold back his usual lopsided grin of delight and failed. "Even the caveman?"

James nodded solemnly. "Especially the caveman." He tightened his hold on Bram. "I love every magnificent, muscled, macho inch of you. And that's a lot to love, caveman."

Basking in the mutual revelation, James dove down and plundered his demanding lover's mouth, matching bruising kiss for bruising kiss, and tongue stroke for tongue stroke, until they were both breathless and panting.

He wrapped his arms around Bram's neck while his lover caressed and kneaded James' back, sides and ass with greedy hands, but exhaustion commanded the moment and neither man was prepared to take their caressing to another level so soon.

Tingling from head to toe with the overload of emotional and physical sensation, James settled himself comfortably beside Bram. They eventually worked themselves into a spoon position with Bram's bulkier frame draped around James, massive chest to slender backside. Silent loving touches replaced words until they both drifted off to sleep.

***

"You don't have to come in. I'll be fine." James shifted in his seat beside Bram and looked at his apartment building out the passenger window of the man's truck.

"I don't mind." Bram parked the truck in front of the building and pocketed his keys, silently communicating his firm intent to accompany James.

"I can handle myself." Exasperated by the big man's attitude, James slipped from the truck. Bram followed, walking around the front of the vehicle to join James. "Williams would have to be nuts to try something again."

"That asshole is nuts." Bram slung an arm over his lover's slender shoulders and they began the short walk to the front entrance.

"Yeah, but--."

"For me, Jamie?" Bram stopped them in their tracks and looked down at James, a beseeching expression on his chiseled face and genuine worry in his eyes. "I need to know you got into your apartment and that everything is all right. Otherwise I'll end up spending the night out here in the truck watching for trouble."

It was the sincere worry in the man's gaze that swayed James. He huffed out a short, tense breath and conceded defeat. "Now, who's nuts?"

Bram grinned. "My nuts are all for you, baby." He

tapped James affectionately on the seat of his pants and winked suggestively at him.

"Oh, for Christ's sake, come on." James jabbed the big man in the ribs and began walking. "I'll never get up in time for work tomorrow if we waste what's left of the night arguing over that jerk." James opened the door and entered the building.

The ride up in the elevator was uneventful except for the searing kiss Bram dropped on James the moment the doors closed. Ruffled and flushed by the time the doors opened, James straightened his clothing and walked out into the hallway, giving Bram a heated glared that wavered between indignation and barely checked lust.

Undaunted, Bram just grinned, hesitating a moment to give James a few paces to decide which way his feelings were headed then gleefully followed his lover out of the elevator.

Several feet ahead, James had just passed by Williams' apartment when the door flew open and man barged out behind James. Williams grabbed James by the arm and swung him around so they were face to face.

The man's cheeks were swollen and bruised, the bridge of his nose bristling with the spiky ends of black sutures embedded in puffy flesh. Even more unpleasant to look at than his face were Williams' eyes. A cruel glare of bitterness was now mixed with a raw lust the man no longer took any pains to hide.

"Don't touch me." James instantly recoiled from the man, yanking his arm out of the man's grip. "You need to leave me alone, Williams."

Williams stepped closer and grunted. "Or what?"

James pushed a finger at the middle of Williams' chest but didn't make physical contact. "Or I'll contact my lawyer, the police and the building superintendent."

James pulled back when he felt Williams lean forward far enough to touch his chest to the pointed finger, but he continued talking. Words had always worked better for James than his fists. "It'll cost you money, time, embarrassment and maybe even your apartment. So back *OFF*!" James pushed at the air between them with both palms facing out and shook his head. "I'm not interested in *anything* from you. Understand?"

Williams flexed his hands at his sides, clenching and unclenching his fists, obviously wanting to touch James. He leaned against the wall by his door and made his voice sound calm and reasonable though the words weren't. "Maybe if I lose my apartment I can come bunk at your place. You're not home much lately." He smiled. To James it was nothing more than a leering, ugly grimace. "I'd love to sleep in your bed."

In one stride, Bram was at Williams' side, flipping the man back to slam his shoulder blades against the wall. "If you don't wise up and leave him alone," Bram braced one arm beside Williams' head and leaned down until he was inches from Williams' startled face, "the next thing you'll be sleeping on could be a metal slab. You know, the kind they have at the city morgue." Bram tapped the end of the man's broken nose with one fingertip. "Understand me?"

Flinching, color seeped from Williams' cheeks and his breathing turned shallow. Swallowing hard he jerked his head to one side in a stilted nod of silent agreement.

Bram waited a beat then straightened, removing his arm from blocking Williams' retreat into his apartment. The other man didn't even glance at James, only sparing a simmering glare of hatred at Bram before disappearing behind his door. The sound of several heavy locks falling into place broke the tension in the air.

Smiling Bram turned around to see an unhappy James waiting for him. "What?"

Silently turning on his heel, James stormed down to his apartment door and let himself in, leaving the door open for Bram as a reluctant after thought. When he heard the door close, James spun around and confronted his lover.

"Why did you do that? I had it under control."

Genuinely surprised, Bram was clearly baffled by James' anger. "Do what? Talk to the guy?"

Putting his hands on both lean hips, James continued to fume. "I had it under control." Pacing back and forth in front of his lover, James alternated his stare between Bram and the hallway behind the wall of his apartment. "Look, you can't be with me twenty-four hours a day, Bram."

Bram lowered his voice and solemnly said, "We're both glad I was here yesterday, Jamie." He reached out and stopped James from pacing, rubbing his hand gently over one of his lover's arms to calm him.

James took a deep steadying breath and nodded. "I know, and yes, you're right, I'm glad you were there, too, then." He looked up at Bram and let the man see the gratitude in his eyes then firmly said, "But I have to fight my own fights whenever I can. I may be smaller than a lot of other guys, but I'm still a grown man."

"Okay." Bram nodded. "I'm sorry." He heaved a sigh of frustration and shook his head. "I don't like the creep. Life has taught me to protect the things I cherish." He placed both hands on James' arms and coaxed him closer. "And that means you."

Leaning into the warmth the big man offered, James rested his hands on Bram's chest and lightly rapped his knuckles against the wall of firm muscle. "I understand that. I even like that." James smirked and lifted his eyebrows. "Actually, I love that about you." But then his voice became serious. "But promise me you won't step in again like that unless I really can't handle the situation on my own. Williams makes me feel helpless enough as it is." A frown marred the smooth skin between his eyebrows and clouded his deep blue, pleading eyes. "Don't you make me feel helpless, too. Okay?"

"Okay. I'll try." Bram breathed in a deep sigh. "But I don't think I'll be very good at it, Jamie. I'm hardwired to protect what's mine." Bram shrugged and looked apologetic. "It's a caveman thing."

"All the guys in the world and I have to fall for a possessive Neanderthal." James reached up to give Bram a forgiving kiss.

Rather than lean down into the kiss, the large man started to lift James off his feet, but paused in mid-lift. A concerned frown marred his handsome face as Bram asked, "Make you feel too helpless if I do this?"

James snickered and held on to the man. "No, Caveman, it'll make me feel tall." He rubbed his tightening groin against Bram's muscular thigh. "And horny."

The frown disappeared and Bram finished lifting James up, bringing their mouths together for a deep, claiming kiss.

Feet dangling off the floor, James pulled back from the rapidly building passion. Wrapping his arms around Bram's stout neck, James made a mental note to set his alarm for an hour earlier than usual before diving back in for more of that demanding kiss, murmuring, "A caveman, lucky me."

Chapter Eight

Bram had reluctantly left James' apartment after a hot and very pleasurable grope session on the couch Sunday night. James had managed to get six hours of sleep before his alarm shattered a stunningly realistic dream he was having about making it with Bram in the bed of the big man's truck.

James' work morning had been full of the usual Monday project status meetings, phone calls and endless cups of coffee, mixed with memories from the weekend that brought a flush to his face and a stirring in his groin at the most inconvenient times.

One particularly lust-filled memory spurred by a sudden deep ache in his backside during a brainstorming session prompted a secretary to ask if he was running a fever. James has shifted uncomfortably onto one hip and blushed a deeper red while claiming the room was too warm for him. It gave him a convenient excuse to loosen his tie and drape his suit coat in his lap over the growing bulge in his pants.

Lunch was take-out James didn't even want. Just as he pushed away the remaining half of his uneaten sandwich, the phone rang. Tempted to ignore it, James let it ring six times before guilt surfaced and he broke down and answered.

Tired and distracted, James let his words out in a breathy sigh. "James Justin, speaking."

"Now that's the voice I've been wanting to hear all day."

The gravelly, velvet tones of his lover shot straight to James' groin and his cock sat up and took notice, as did James. He straightened up in his chair and a smile broke out on his blushing face. "Bram! Hey. I was hoping you'd call. I thought maybe we could have met for lunch."

"Sorry, Jamie. I had something personal to take care of over lunch." Bram's response was distracted and curt then he softened his tone to ask, "What about dinner tonight?"

James blinked at the sudden change, but brushed it off, letting the pleasure of hearing from his lover take over. "Can't. I'm working late. There's a new client coming in. We all have to be on hand for the initial meet and greet. They're flying in this evening and then out to Brussels right after the meeting. This is the only opportunity to get together. It's a huge project."

"Damn. That nixes my plans for the evening. And I have a meeting all day in Chicago tomorrow and I won't be back until late." Bram blew out a deep, huffed breath in frustration. He made a determined effort to salvage the scheduling conflict. "So how about lunch Wednesday? Meet me at noon, at the corner of Fifth and Lyell."

"Fifth and Lyell? There isn't anything there but a couple of office buildings and a construction site."

"Right. It's my site. I'll bring lunch. You can meet a few of the boys and get to see what I'm working on first hand. Mitch has been yanking my chain about you all day. I think it's only fair you get to share in the abuse, too."

James could hear the bright smile on Bram's face over the line. "Mitch? He was the one at the bar with you Friday night, wasn't he?"

"Yep. He's accusing me of robbing the cradle. Thinks you're too young and good looking for me."

Snorting out a half-laugh, James grinned. "If what you say about Mitch's taste in women is true, I think I've just been insulted in some weird-ass, backhanded way."

Bram laughed, a contagious, deep, rolling sound that made James' ass flutter and clench, as sizzling sparks of want and desire gathered in his groin. The big man's voice was liquid sex, flowing around James like an electric current, snapping and sizzling at his nerve sensors.

A loud voice yelled for Bram in the background and James heard the other man cover the phone with his hand and yell an obscenity back then uncover the phone again.

"So we're meeting for lunch Wednesday." The casual, but businesslike tone dropped from Bram's voice, and became sultry and inviting. "I want to see you, Jamie. Two days is too long to go without my being able to touch you. Maybe we can make a little time for some one-on-one after lunch." His voice left no question about what sport Bram was thinking of, and it wasn't basketball.

"Sounds interesting and ambitious." James found his voice had gone raspy with desire. Bram responded to it like bull to a red flag.

"Like I said Friday night, I like a challenge, baby." They shared a moment of heavy breathing in which James relived the moment in the bar when Bram had said that to him and then proceed to win the pool game, the bet and James' body, followed closely by his heart and soul.

"Christ, Bram. I can't wait to see you." James ran a hand over the growing bugle in his pants and glanced at his closed office door. "Listening to your voice and not getting to touch you is torture."

"I know, Jamie. I miss your sweet ass, too." Taking a deep breath, Bram promised, "We'll make plans for the whole weekend Wednesday, too. I have tickets to something I think you'll like for Friday night." The voice in the background yelled again. "Listen, Jamie, I have to go. I'll call you after my meeting in Chicago. I'll even bring you home a present. Good luck with your new client tonight. I love you. Miss you, baby. Stay safe for me, Jamie."

The line went dead before James could do more than stutter out a quick "I love you, too. Be careful." James leaned back and let his half-hard erection slowly subside.

The day ended with another less anticipated phone call. The moment the line lit up, James knew who it was. He had been dreading the call all day. Overhearing Art and his secretary discussing the subject over lunch, he knew what to expect. James imagined as a junior architect and low man on the totem pole at work, his call would come at the end of the day.

Suppressing a heavy sigh, he answered the phone. "James Justin speaking."

"James, Philip Dunn here. Good afternoon."

"Good afternoon, sir."

"By now you've probably heard I've been following up on the dinner invitations at my home for this Friday night."

"I haven't forgotten, sir."

"I take it we can make room for two more at the table then, James?"

James imagined the look that would be on Mrs. Dunn's face if he showed up with another man to her formal, socialite dinner party. "Can I get back to you on that, Mr. Dunn?"

James broke out in a cold sweat. His career was very important to him. Before Bram came along, it was all he had to depend on. But Bram had spent an entire afternoon introducing his 'boyfriend' to his neighbors and friends and had made it clear he wanted to be involved in James' day-to-day life.

"Of course, my boy. There's no rush."

"Thank you, sir."

"You know, James, alone or with a friend, I look forward to seeing you there. *Dunn & Piper* is a close knit company, son. I like to get to know my most promising junior associates."

"Ah, well, thank you, Mr. Dunn. I don't know what to say."

"Just say you'll be there."

"Yes, sir. I'll be there."

"Fine, fine. My wife will be pleased to hear it, too, James."

"I-I'll have to get back to you about whether I'll be bringing someone or not."

"You do that, James. I'll see you at tonight's client meeting. Good afternoon."

"Yes, sir. Good afternoon, sir."

Staring at the now silent receiver, James replaced the phone and slowly dropped his head to the draftsman desk in front of him and repeatedly banged his forehead on the tilted surface.

The specter of Friday night's formal with his co-workers and his boss suddenly became so much more than just an office dinner party.

Greeted by Williams' bruised and sneering face watching from the doorway to the man's apartment when he arrive home, Monday night was spent tossing and turning, looking for a familiar warm body. Only four days of knowing Bram and James was already missing the man.

***

Tuesday morning lumbered by at an extraordinarily slow pace. James' e-mail had contained a surprise message from Bram detailing the big man's meeting schedule and flight plan in Chicago. James didn't know how Bram got his e-mail address, but he was delighted to see the message when he checked his mail in the morning. He devoted his morning break to fantasizing about being in a lavish hotel suite with his assertive new lover.

By midmorning, James was tempted to escape to the bathroom and relieve the growing ache in his neglected groin with a little personal attention, but the thoughts of satisfying his needs by himself left him feeling frustrated and lonely. Thankfully, his workload and visits from needy colleagues refocused his mind on his work and out of his pants.

By lunchtime, James finally admitted to himself he was craving his absent partner. Less than a week into this unexpected relationship and James was lost. Bram had claimed him, heart, soul and body. He didn't want to think about a day when he wouldn't see or talk to this man. He realized how happy he'd felt after Bram's call yesterday.

The big man's voice had the power to make James feel protected and secure, just like his massive presence did. James found it all confusing and frightening, as well as deeply thrilling. He had never felt this attached to someone so quickly before.

James thought about Bram's work roughened hands and demanding mouth touching, taking, claiming, him again and again. The dull, yearning ache returned to his groin and his cock stirred.

Tempted again to take care of the growing problem, James made the decision to visit the men's room just as the phone rang. He hesitated, considering ignoring it just this once then gave in and answered the call. The honey laced, deep voice on the other end of the line caused his partial erection to immediately harden.

"Hey, Jamie."

"Bram, hi! You read my mind. I was just thinking about you."

"That's encouraging."

James cleared his throat and twisted in his seat. "Kind of missing you." He gnawed on his lower lip and fought the urge to slip his hand under the waistband of his pants. The deep, seductive Voice on the other end of the line was doing interesting things to his libido and his anatomy.

The Voice dropped an octave lower, turning sultry and provocative. "Miss you too, baby. Been thinking about you since I left your place Sunday. The weekend was too short. Way too short. You need to pack a bag and leave a few things at my place so we don't have to separate so early on work days."

Nodding, James played with the button above his fly. "Yeah, yeah, I think I'll do that. It would have been nice to have had another night together."

"It'd be nice to have all my nights with you, baby, even if we just slept. I love waking up with your sweet little ass pressed against me." The sound of cloth rustling came over the line. "Your skin is so warm and smooth, nestled up against my chest and pressing back on my cock. I can hardly keep myself from ramming it home before you're even awake." The distinctive noise a zipper makes came over the phone next.

"God, Bram." James squirmed a little more in his chair, his pants tenting, his cock straining against the soft fabric of his boxers. "You're making it impossible for me to sit here and keep my hands off myself."

"Then don't." The reply was simple and direct.

"What?" James' voice rose along with his eyebrows.

"Touch yourself, Jamie." The Voice was silky smooth and deep. "Pretend it's my hand holding your cock, stroking you."

"Christ, Bram. You're going to make me crazy." James looked desperately at the open office door to be sure no one was near it. A note of panic tinged his voice. "I'm at work!"

"Close the door. You're by yourself, aren't you?" The Voice made it sound like the most reasonable thing in the world.

"Yeah, but --." The panic was replaced with uncertainty and a touch of interest.

"Close the door, baby." The persuasive Voice was thick with desire. "Do it now." Bram's words had a commanding, biting edge to them that made James' cock quiver.

"Okay." James' own voice was shaky and feathery light. "Hang on a minute." He awkwardly walked across the room to the office door and closed and locked it. "'Kay," came the breathy reply, "it's closed."

"All alone, now?"

James returned to his chair and glanced nervously around the small office. "Yeah, it's just you, me and the Phone Company."

Bram laughed. "An audience, that's something new." The rich, throaty sound sparked bursts of excitement in James' groin, and his chest tightened when a tingling sensation shot up his spine.

"Don't get excited, Caveman." James chuckled but put a note of seriousness into his words. "This is as public as I get."

A rumbling growl carried through the phone. "Don't worry, baby, I don't share. You're mine. All mine. Just mine." The Voice was playfully threatening and dark. "I think we established that over the weekend."

James lightly rubbed over the tender, deep purple area on his shoulder. "Your teeth marks are still there, if that's what you mean."

"Actually, I meant my cum I put up your tight, sweet ass, baby. Buried my cock next to your heart and wrote on it with my juice. You're mine now." The voice purred, satisfied and smug. "Take your cock out and stroke it for me, baby."

James' engorged cock jerked and strained against his shorts. He could feel the warm wetness on the tip as it began to leak.

"Jesus, Bram."

James' hands popped the button of his waistband and his zipper was down before he consciously though about what he was doing. James pulled his cock free and began stroking the hot flesh, eyes closed; phone pressed so hard against his ear he could hear cartilage creak. The vision of Bram the way he looked in the shower on Sunday bloomed behind James' closed eyes and he groaned. He blocked out the rest of the world and concentrated on listening to his lover's hypnotic voice.

"That's it. Stroke yourself, baby. Run your hand up

that hot, hard rod and jerk it back down, hard." James groaned again and his sharp, needy gasp made the Voice chuckle. "Again and again." James gulped and licked at his dry lips, panting. "Now take it to the top and swirl your thumb over the head." The Voice rumbled again, saturated with undeniable lust. "I wish I could taste you, baby. Lick that cum right off that shiny cock head and swallow you whole."

James moaned and then whimpered as bright flashes of desire shot through his cock and sizzled up his spine to set off a series of mini fireworks in his brain.

The Voice never stopped, relentless in its goal to bring him off over the phone. "Rub that thick, delicious cream over it. Are you doing it, baby? Can you feel me touching you with my big, rough hands?"

James gasped and muttered, "Oh, fuck!"

"I'll take that as a yes." The humor faded from the Voice. It was throaty and rough, like honey on sandpaper, excitement and need clear in Bram's commanding tone. "I have big hands, so big I can reach right down there between your legs and cup your balls," James automatically leaned back in his chair and spread his legs at the unspoken command, "and still reach that sweet, tight, little hole of yours with my fingers. I love to push right into that cherry ass, love to feel you squeezing and clinging to me, trying to pull me right inside of you."

James hunched lower in his seat and fingered his sac with his other hand, his breath coming in sharp little gasps.

The Voice purred and panted. "You are so fucking hot just touching you makes my blood boil and my brain fry. All I can think about is having you, burying my cock so deep I can feel your heart beating." The Voice was getting strained and more labored.

James could hear the sound of flesh sliding over flesh from Bram's end of the line. Just imagining the big man jerking off to the music of his grunts and groans nearly made James cum all on its own.

"I can, you know," the Voice whispered, "feel your heartbeat when I'm deep inside of you, baby. Feels like your heart's stroking me, pulsing against me, pounding back at me in that gentle way you have. Making me love you, fuck you, making me want to fucking stay inside you forever." Both men groaned. "You and your hot, tight ass, clinging and milking my long, hard rod until I cream your little hole," the Voice quivered and went deeper, grunting out the next words between gritted teeth, "and fill you up with my load of juice." A hoarse drawn out grunt followed by heavy breathing told James Bram had found release.

Knowing he had caused the big man to cum sent a buzz of delight through James, making his chest ache and his cock jump. An electric shiver raced through his entire body and he exploded, visions of a spurting Bram dancing behind his closed eyes.

"Fuck!" James bucked his hips in the air and let out a strangled cry as his cock throbbed, pulsing out a load of thick cum. He jerked forward and forced the majority of it to land on the floor between his spread legs, salvaging most of his dress pants from the creamy shower.

As he jerked up, the phone slipped from where he had it clamped between shoulder and chin. It landed on the floor with a thud. He grabbed a tissue from a box on the corner of his desk and wrestled his fading cock back inside his pants while he scrabbled under his desk for the phone.

"Bram? Hang on, I dropped the phone," James

called out as he crawled further under his desk and snagged the handset off the floor. He wiggled back into the open and rose to his knees. "Got it. Sorry, hope I didn't rupture an ear drum for you."

"You made something burst, but it wasn't my ear drum, baby." Bram's voice was still tight and breathless, but there was a smile in it. "Your voice keeps fading in and out. Where are you?"

"Getting up from the floor."

"Are you on your knees?" The Voice was back. "Because I can picture you on your knees between my legs, baby, all naked and hot, getting ready to taste my cock."

James squirmed and grabbed his twitching cock through his pants. "Stop right now! I don't have the energy to do that again so soon!"

Bram snorted and let loose a long, gravelly laugh of delight.

A sudden unexpected wave of loneliness made James' throat tighten up. His voice shook as he stumbled over the conversation. "That *was* something else, Bram. I've never had phone sex before. I'll have to appreciate the phone company more after this."

"I take it this 'threesome' was good for you, too?" A dry chuckle and a sigh of contentment transmitted over the line from Bram's end.

James laughed and pulled himself up off the floor, rearranging and tucking his clothing back into place as he stood. "Yeah, it was fabulous." His tone turned softer and more sincere. "You're unbelievable." James' voice hitched. "I-I miss you."

"Miss you too, baby." Bram's tone was full of longing and determination. "I'll be home by ten

Wednesday morning and you're going to meet me for lunch at the site by eleven. Why don't you pack a bag and plan on spending the night at the house after work? We'll have more time to spend together that way."

It made a big statement to James to have his own toothbrush in someone else's bathroom and his clothes lying in a drawer beside another man's things. It said commitment and that scared James more than just a little. James swallowed down his reservations.

"I'll pack a few things, sure." James pulled in a deep breath and forced himself to think of the pleasures that came with the commitment. "I'm looking forward to seeing you, too." James brushed his hand over his still tingling cock and sighed. "Nobody kisses the way you do, Caveman."

Bram chuckled again and huffed out his own sigh of frustration. "You just remember what it felt like the last time to have my tongue down your throat and my cock up your ass pounding your sweet cheeks and I promise to make that memory pale in comparison to how I'll make you feel when I get home." The dark and dangerous, possessive tone was back in his voice.

James shivered, every cell of his body registering the commanding, claiming tone and responding to it, yearning for it. Before James' brain had a chance to catch up with his libido, his mouth responded, too. "You'll have to catch me before you can take me, Caveman. Drag me back to your lair. Reclaim me. If you can." Surprised at the teasing, provocative tone and his own choice of goading words, James made a pained face and closed his eyes, waiting for an angry response from Bram.

Instead, a deep, amused snort reached James' ears. "Why you little flirt." A deep grunt drifted across the line.

"My cock hasn't gotten this hard this soon after shooting off in years." Clothing rustled again in the background. "You can bet your sweet ass I'll reclaim it *and* your sassy mouth. You'll remember who you belong to for a long, long time when I'm done with you, baby."

"Make that a promise." James cringed. First he's afraid of leaving a few things at Bram's house then he's challenging the man to make him forget about any other lover. James decided the frequent, mind-blowing sex with this man must have been short-circuiting his brain cells.

"It's more than a promise, baby, it's a fact. Count on it."

"Good. I want to. I-I am."

Bram spit out each word like it was a bullet with James' name on it, all of them headed straight for James' heart. "Then count on this, too, Jamie. I love you."

James' voice quivered and dropped to a reverent whisper. "Love you, too."

"Good. Then we're both right were we need to be."

"Yeah, yeah, we're good."

Voices sounded outside of James' door and he hurried over to unlock it before anyone tried the handle, the phone clutched tightly to his ear. He made it back to his drafting table just as knock tapped on the door and it popped open. Art stuck his head in the room and motioned at James, pointing at his watch and making a 'come on' gesture with both hands. James suddenly remembered his afternoon meeting.

James pointed at the phone and turned his back on the waiting man. "Ah, listen. I have to go. I'm late for a meeting with the boss. I'm really glad you called."

"Me too, Jamie. Phone calls won't be the same from now on. I'll always be imagining you jerking off at the other end of the line. Could make calling my shareholders a little tough."

James laughed and covertly checked to be sure that his zipper was up, feeling a blush race up his cheeks to his hairline. "Thanks for that image, Bram. Now I can't use the phone the same way ever again either."

"James!" Art called in aloud stage whisper, tapping the crystal of his watch again.

Sighing, James nodded in Art's general direction, but kept focused on Bram. "I have to go. Be safe coming home and I'll see you tomorrow. Bye."

"Bye, Jamie. See you soon, baby."

Hanging up the phone, James gave Art a sour glare. The other man just leered and punched James in the arm as they left the room. "Was that a date I just heard you making, James?"

"Maybe."

"New boyfriend? Are you bringing him to the dinner party Friday?" Art took in the unhappy closed look on James' face. "Dunn won't care, James. At least, I don't think he will. He's pretty open-minded."

"Maybe, but I'm not sure about everyone else that's going to be there." James closed the door to his office and trailed after Art, mumbling to himself along the way. "Including me."

Chapter Nine

A long, lonely evening passed for James, brightened only by the absence of Williams. James treaded very softly past the man's apartment door and was embarrassed to admit feeling relieved when it didn't open as he passed.

Wanting to ask Bram to go with him to the dinner party Friday night, but terrified of his boss's and co-workers reaction if he showed up with the big man as his boyfriend, James' night was a restless one. His dreams were filled with mind-blowing erotic scenes from every tryst he and Bram had over the last five days, mixed with stomach-churning memories of harsh words and condemning rants from his family.

By morning, James was exhausted and on edge. The only thing that kept him from calling in sick and staying in bed with the covers over his head was the prospect of seeing Bram for lunch. With that pleasant thought in mind, James dragged himself to the shower and started his day, skipping breakfast out of fear of throwing it up. Dinner the night before had been two bites of a cold ham sandwich and three cups of reheated, twelve-hour old coffee. He resigned himself to the fact nausea was undoubtedly going to be his constant companion for the day.

Once James arrived at the office the morning actually moved very fast, consumed by a looming deadline on the newest project the group he worked with had been handed Monday night. Ten-thirty and time to meet Bram for lunch came so fast James didn't have the opportunity to get nervous.

Throwing on his coat, James left the building, excited and preoccupied with thoughts of his new lover.

Bram was almost obsessed with having James meet the people in his life. It was like the big man wanted to pull James into his world as quickly as he could and surround James with the security of it, make him comfortable in it, so James wouldn't think about leaving.

Not that he'd thought about it. Leaving was the last thing James wanted, but he wasn't sure he had the strength to stay. It made James' head spin when he thought about it. He hadn't met this many new people and done this many different things in such a short period of time in his life. It was scary, but he had to admit having Bram by his side made it all seem normal.

What was normal anyway? Afternoon walks and dinners out James had done before on dates, but wild, earth-shattering sex in alleyways, restaurants and on kitchen countertops was something new for him. It was crazy, but if going crazy meant the greatest sex of his life with a god-like lover the size of Mt. Olympus, who happened to be a terrific, loving guy besides, then James was willing to go completely insane.

The drive over to the work site took twenty minutes. James found an empty parking spot near what looked like a project trailer. Walking toward the fenced in area, James saw several men dressed in grime-coated work clothes milling around inside of the gate. Most wore heavy jeans and work shirts with suspenders, and thick leather tool belts around their hips. All of them had bright yellow hard hats on. All of them were muscular, beefy men, even the shorter, heavier ones, the smallest of them overshadowing James by fifty pounds and several inches. All of the men turned and watched as James approached them, his pleated trousers, white shirt and tie, and tailored trench coat making him feel all the more out of place.

The stares were friendly, but curious. Weaving a path through the group, James smiled and nodded. He neared the steps to the trailer when one worker stepped forward and cut off his path, bringing James up short, nose to chest with a faded blue denim shirt opened to reveal a sweat-soaked T-shirt underneath. James brought his gaze up and looked the man in the eye, noting the faint scar over his left cheek and the graying ponytail loosely draped over a shoulder.

A vague sense of familiarity touched James. Squinting at the human roadblock, James searched his memory for a name. "Have we met?"

The man stared a moment longer than grunted. "Kinda. We didn't meet, exactly, but I saw you at the bar last Friday. At the pool table." Mitch slowly looked James over from head to toe and back again, then grinned. "I left with the barmaid." He winked at the man beside him then leered at James. "You left with the boss man."

A round of soft chuckles from knowing faces came out of the increasing circle of men, but none sounded cruel or jeering. James relaxed slightly and considered his answer carefully.

"Ah. You must be Mitch. Bram told me about your legendary taste in women." Mitch beamed and preened, running a rough, chapped hand over his unkempt mustache. "But he did suggest that half the time he didn't know if you were dating or dog sitting."

Another round of laughter erupted from the

group, but this time the men were laughing with him. The fierce blush on his face took some of the edge off his reply, but James felt he had given almost as good as he had gotten. He held his breath when the look on Mitch's face froze.

Mitch stared at James for the longest ten seconds of James' life then dissolved into a fit of laughter. He pounded James on the back. The momentum almost knocked the smaller man off his feet. Mitch slung an arm around James' shoulders, hugging him to his side.

"You got balls for a little guy. I guess if the boss has decided to subject you to these animals," Mitch gestured at the assembled men behind him, throwing the finger when several loud growls and howls answered him, "he must really like you."

Mitch nudged the man to his left with an elbow. "Hey Marty. Go tell the man it's time to eat, his lunch is here." Mitch loosed his hold on James and chuckled. "I mean his lunch *date* is here."

James blushed a deeper red. Before he could think of a rebuttal, a smooth, deep voice from behind them answered for him.

"You could only wish to be so lucky at lunch time, Mitch." Bram walked towards them from out of a large tent pitched at the end of the trailer and separated Mitch from James. James couldn't keep the bright smile that pulled at his mouth from dominating his entire face at the sight of his lover.

"And hands off. He's not your type. He's too good looking for you." Bram rubbed a large palm over James' shoulder and smiled down at him, his voice soft and welcoming. "Hey, Jamie. You made it. It's good to see you."

"Hi, Bram. Welcome home."

The hungry expression in Bram's eyes made James' skin tingle and he shivered as an electric burst of pleasure raced up his spine. The small shudder transmitted to Bram's hand on James' shoulder and the big man's eyes dilated with lust in response. James fought the urge to pant, licking his suddenly dry lips and delighting in the way Bram's gaze flickered down to watch his mouth. James became conscious of the stares and quiet smirks all around him and he bit at his lower lip.

The small, nervous gesture didn't go unnoticed by his intuitive lover. Bram broke his adoring gaze and casually turned James toward the tent. "Let's have lunch and I'll introduce you to these heathens then show you around the site. The animal pack here can tell you what they're up to at each pod."

Bram slung and arm around James' shoulder and beamed proudly at his work force and friends and growled. "Jamie is an architect, so don't try to dazzle him with your bullshit. He'll make mincemeat out of all of you grunts." There were a number of half-hearted and playful grumbles from the men, but Bram ignored them.

He jerked his chiseled, clean-shaven chin in his construction friend's direction. "Mitch, find Jamie a hard hat for later, will you?" His gaze returned to James' face and his expression softened. "I want to make damn sure nothing bad happens to him." He winked at James.

James smiled at the lopsided grin on the man's love-struck face, just barely catching Bram's final, whispered word that made his heart race. "Forever."

***

Energized by lunch, Bram's company, and promises of an active and interesting night at Bram's house ahead of him, James returned to the office and plunged back into his work. By four o'clock, James was deep into the groove, designing, planning, and brainstorming ideas with two other architects, exchanging ideas and making and accepting numerous calls on fact finding missions from within the company.

So when the phone rang for the umpteenth time, he didn't bother with pleasantries, answering with a distracted grunt. "Yeah? James, here."

"Mr. James Justin? Apartment 4C in the Butler Building on West 12th Street?" The voice was sharp, disapproving and female.

"Yeah, that's me." James couldn't decide whether to be worried or just curious. "Who is this?"

"This is Mrs. Susan Fibbs, one of your building superintendents." Her tone reflected she thought he should already be aware of her identity.

"Oh." James settled on being confused and curious. "Well, hello, Mrs. Fibbs. What can I do for you?"

"I'm calling regarding a complaint we've had from one of our other tenants." The sharpness took on a prim edge.

"A complaint? About me?" James lost interest in the layout he had been studying for the first part of the conversation and concentrated on the women at the other end of the line. "I'm afraid I don't understand."

"Not about you, per se, Mr. Justin. About your 'friend'." Mrs. Fibbs managed to put just enough emphasis on the word 'friend' to make it sound dirty.

"My 'friend'?" James let her know he understood her prejudicial inference.

"The very large friend you have been, shall we say, 'keeping company with'?"

"You mean Bram?" James hesitated for a just a moment before adding, "My boyfriend?"

"Yes, well." Mrs. Fibbs cleared her throat, her tone flustered and irritated. "Whatever he is, we've received a very serious complaint from Mr. Williams in apartment 4A about him. As your 'guest', you are responsible for his behavior."

"He's not a guest, he's my boyfriend, Mrs. Fibbs."

"Very well, if you insist." Mrs. Fibbs huffed, irritated at having to use words she found distasteful. "Mr. Williams claims your 'boyfriend' assaulted him and invaded his home, threatening more bodily harm on two more occasions, all in the past week." Her voice became mildly outraged. "The poor man had a very impressive array of injuries, Mr. Justin, very impressive indeed. Your 'boyfriend' must be a brute!"

James worked to keep his voice calm. "First of all, Mrs. Fibbs, Bram is *not* a brute. He's a kind, wonderful man. He was protecting *me* from an assault by Williams."

"So he is responsible for the man's injuries. I knew it." Her tone left no question she considered the matter closed.

"Let me explain the situation, Mrs. Fibbs. It's not what it seems."

"I've heard enough. The man assaulted a tenant and then harassed him in his home on two additional occasions. We have the safety of all the building's occupants to think of, Mr. Justin. It's obvious having you and your type of 'friends' in the building is an unacceptable risk."

"Bram has only interacted with Williams twice and

both times were to protect me." A nagging sense of unease nudged at James' insecurities. Bram had said he couldn't meet him for lunch on Monday because he'd had 'something personal to take care of'. Could he have gone to see Williams without James knowing about it? Would Bram have broken his promise to let James handle the situation? "Mrs. Fibbs, if you'd just let me explain --."

"I'm sorry Mr. Justin, but we'll be issuing you a sixty day eviction notice as of today. There are small children living on your floor, Mr. Justin. We have to think of the children."

"Williams is keeping pitbulls in his apartment, Mrs. Fibbs! How safe is that for 'the children'?"

"How dangerous can they be? They didn't stop your brute of a boyfriend from inflicting injury on the poor man. No, Mr. Justin, the eviction notice stands."

"Mrs. Fibbs!"

"Good day, sir."

James stared at the silent phone in his hand then replaced it on the base. "Christ. I've managed to lose my sense of self-preservation, my perspective, my identity, my heart *and* my apartment all in one week."

James pushed off the desk as he jumped from his seat. He walked right past his coat and out the door, slamming it as he strode down the hall. "Now I hope I don't lose the only thing that really matters."

***

Bram's truck was parked in front of the office trailer, but the man was seven stories up and out on a steel girder when James returned to the construction site. The foreman radioed him he had a visitor again and Bram began the long descent to the ground. James spotted the man high up on the skeletal structure, but he couldn't watch the powerfully built, athletic man jump from narrow steel beam to beam without wanting to throw up.

The sharp breeze cut through James' dress shirt and fluttered his tie around his neck. He hunched his shoulders against the increasing cold and paced back and forth beside the truck, drawing curious glances from several of the workers. By the time Bram made it to the ground, James had worked himself up into a cold sweat despite the falling temperatures.

Bram hit the ground floor at a hurried pace. His vest flapped in the wind, jeans dust-covered and hair sweaty and out of place from the tight band inside the hardhat. He tossed the bright yellow hat and his tool belt onto a nearby bench as he passed it, never breaking stride or taking his concerned gaze off of a shivering James.

Eyebrows knitted together in confusion, Bram strode over. "Jamie? What's the matter?" Seeing James coatless and freezing, he slipped out of his own down-filled vest and tried to wrap it around James. "Where's your coat?"

"I forgot it." Shrugging off Bram's attempts to warm him up, James pushed Bram's hands away. "That's not important."

"Well, it should be." Bram open the truck's passenger door and pulled a quilted flannel shirt from behind the seat. "And it is to me. It's forty-two degrees out here, Jamie." He tossed it to James, who automatically caught it.

Gripping the bulky shirt in both hands, James' knuckles turned white. "I have to ask you something, Bram." He twisted the shirt, strangling the fabric. James felt lost and hurt, anticipating an answer he didn't want to hear, but was sure he would. "I don't want to," he blinked against the sting of unshed tears, "but I have to."

Looking even more confused than before, Bram slowly nodded. "Okay. I don't have anything to hide, Jamie."

James paced and distractedly mauled Bram's shirt. The moment his lower lip was sucked between his teeth, he began to gnaw on it hard enough to rake a layer of chapped skin off.

Bram knew this was serious. "Just ask me."

"Did you go see Williams Monday, on your own?" James' words were fast-paced and hitched between tight little gasps of breath. "When you said you couldn't get together for lunch?"

"What?" Bram's mouth dropped open and his clenched fists rested on his hips.

James' voice went an octave higher and several nearby workmen stopped what they were doing to listen. "Did you go harass Williams?" His pace slowed and James stopped in front of Bram. "At his apartment? Behind my back."

"Behind your *back*?" The extra emphasis Bram put on the last word accented how incredulous he felt.

"I have to know, Bram!" James was shouting now and his pacing resumed at a frenzied rate. He stopped every few words to slap a palm against Bram's broad, heaving chest. "Did you break your promise? Did you just decide that how I wanted to handle the problem wasn't important and take over?"

"When would I have done that?" Bram glanced down at the small hand periodically thumping on his sternum, but ignored it otherwise. "And *why* would I have done it?"

"Monday! When you said you had something personal to take care of?" James worked himself into a fevered pitch, terrified he was losing Bram, but helpless to stop himself from forcing the man farther away. "You never said what you were doing, but it was important enough to you to keep from seeing me one more time before you left town."

"Why you egotistical, little shit." Bram moved closer, his eyes narrowed and his breaths coming in angry deep, controlled huffs.

Mindless of the significant differences in their sizes, James pushed at Bram again. Silent, Bram allowed himself to be shoved back an inch or two. "This isn't about me, damn it! It's about you! Us! And about whether or not you're going to try and run my life!"

Bram reacted instinctively to the growing panic in James' shaky voice and wide eyes. He grabbed James by the shoulder, keeping him in place. "What's this all about, really, Jamie?"

Trying to regain his control, James closed his eyes and took several deep breaths then looked up at Bram. "It's about my getting a call this afternoon from my building's superintendent complaining about you!" His moment of control deserted him. "It's about my losing my apartment!"

"Your apartment? Why?" James jerked under Bram's restraining hand and Bram tightened his hold.

"Williams." James spit out the name like it was venom. "He told the building superintendents you went to his place and threatened him a third time." James pulled out of Bram's grip and began pacing again. "You promised you'd let me handle it! You promised me you wouldn't interfere!"

Shaking his head, Bram threw his hands up in frustration. "I *didn't*, Jamie."

James stopped and got up into Bram's face. "Then where did you go Monday?" He thumped the hand holding the mangled shirt against Bram's tense shoulder. "What was so important? Why won't you just tell me?"

Voice deadly calm and measured, Bram's jaw set into a grim line. "It's very personal."

Outraged James missed the hard glint in Bram's eye. "Personal! Personal!" James slapped Bram's chest with both hands, but the big man didn't budge an inch this time. James didn't notice. He shouted up at Bram's closed, guarded face. "You tell me you love me and want to spend all our time together, but you can't tell me something 'personal'?"

Never-ending shivers began to quake through James' slender body, but he didn't notice them. He backed away from Bram, rapidly shaking his head. His curls flew in his face, aided by the increasing cold winds. "That's not going to cut it, Bram. Not by a long shot."

Tears welled in his eyes and his voice hitched, but his tone was determined. "I can't stay with someone who'll betray my trust. I've have enough of that my life."

James turned to walk away, head down and shoulders hunched then realized he was still holding Bram's shirt. He turned sideways and thrust it at Bram, in a hurry to walk away and not let the man see the extent of his anguish.

Instead of the shirt being taken, James' wrist was encased in a firm, leather-covered grip. Bram tightened his fingers and yanked James closer, pulling the smaller man off his feet. He loomed over James, his face set in a mask of tense control, his eyes flashing with scorching anger.

"Oh, no you don't, Jamie." Bram moved them both the five feet to the truck. He opened the passenger door with one hand while keeping a grip on James with the other.

"You can't just come here and accuse me of lying to you, betraying you, and then just walk away like our relationship doesn't mean anything." Bram shoved James toward the open cab. "You want to know what I was doing on Monday so badly, what I didn't want to weigh you down with yet, then I'll show you." He pointed over James' shoulder at the bench seat, his voice curt and unquestioningly authoritative. "Get in the truck."

Desperately glad Bram wasn't going to let him walk away without an explanation, but afraid to say so, James moved slowly.

Just like he had on the first night they met, Bram grabbed James by the waist and tossed him into the cab. Before slamming the door shut, Bram pointed an accusing finger at him. "And put on the fucking shirt! Your god damn lips are turning blue!"

Settling onto the leather seat, James didn't utter a word of complaint. He slipped the too big shirt on and hugged the thick fabric to his body, wrapping it around and crossing it over itself to seal in any body heat he might have left. Suddenly aware of how cold he really was, James began shaking so hard his teeth chattered. Not wanting to upset Bram further, he pulled his lips between his teeth to deaden the sound.

Walking around the truck, Bram looked over his shoulder at the men nearby. "Mitch, tell Eddie I've gone. I'll call him later and check on the schedule for tomorrow."

"You got it, boss." Mitch's voice was an attempt at

neutrality, but even James could hear the genuine c
in it.

James silently groaned realizing Mitch and two other workmen had been standing several feet away during the entire conversation. He had been so worked up his natural abhorrence for public displays had taken a backseat to getting a straight answer from Bram. James slouched and pulled the collar of the shirt higher around his face.

Bram swung up into the driver's seat, slammed the door shut and started the truck. After one look at James' shuddering body, he reached over and gently, but firmly, pulled an unresisting James closer to his own furnace-like body. Next he adjusted the cab heater on full blast.

Throughout it all, Bram was silent, a simmering anger radiating off him. Throwing his arm over the back of the seat, he backed out of the parking area. After putting the truck into drive, he let his arm curl around James' still quaking shoulders and headed south.

At the construction lot, Mitch watched the truck's taillights fade into traffic then tossed the cigarette he was smoking to the ground. He glanced up at the two men beside him and tipped his head to one side in thought. "Well, whadaya know, boys. Looks like the boss got himself a real little spitfire."

The tall, red-haired man to his left snorted. "Got balls, that's for sure. Haven't seen anyone try to shove the boss around in years. Not since that drunk over in Avon last Christmas." Buck smiled at the memory. "Bet that guy's still talking soprano."

Buck ground out the stogy he was dragging on and put the remainder in his pocket. "Gotta give the little bastard credit, though. The boss usually has to pry his dates off with a crowbar."

The third man, Mike, chuckled, pulling his outer shirt closer against the rising winds. "Never heard of one of them trying to break up with him before. Gold diggers never want to give up a catch like Abraham Lord."

Mitch stared down the road after his childhood friend. Finally, a smile cracked his bearded, weathered face. "'Bout time the pushy bastard found somebody willing to walk away if the boss wasn't treating him right."

Grunting, Mitch resettled the hard hat on his head and started walking back to the work site. "That damn dick-loving, thick-headed mountain better not screw it up. Be a fucking shame if he lost this one."

Mitch slapped Buck on the back and stepped into the waiting service elevator. "'Sides, I kinda like the squirt. All those curls and big blue eyes, he looks like one of those poodle things they used to put inside teacups. Ya know?"

Snickering, Buck nodded. "Kinda yips and bites at the boss like one, too."

The three burly men entertained themselves by making high-pitched puppy noises, laughing all the way to the top of the incomplete building.

Chapter Ten

The drive to the south end of town was quiet with only the droning hum of the tires and the buzz of the cab heater invading the tense mood. Ten miles out Bram turned onto a less traveled, quiet road.

Two miles later, a large institutional building came into view. Just before they turned into the building's driveway, a large sign greeted them. It read 'Dunnhill Rehabilitation and Treatment Center'.

Still under Bram's arm, James was more relaxed, but confused. "What are we doing here?"

"You wanted to know where I was Monday." Bram nodded at the building. "I'm showing you." His grave expression and the sudden sadness in his voice made James tense.

"At a hospital?"

"Yeah. I usually spend every Sunday afternoon here." Bram pulled into the lot and parked the truck. "This past Sunday, I was with you." He stared down at James and his anger drained away. "So, instead, I came on Monday."

Looking from Bram to the hospital and back again, James' forehead wrinkled and he frowned. "Why?"

Briefly caressing the soft flyaway curls at the base of James' neck, Bram climbed out of the truck. He gestured for James to come out his side as well. "Come on, I'll show you."

Bewildered, James followed, Bram's flannel shirt engulfing and dwarfing his body, making him look and feel ten years old. He wiped a sleeve over his eyes to erase any dried tears. The lingering scent of the shirt's owner filled his nostrils, sending a spark of excitement through his senses. James pushed the nerve tingling sensation to the back of his mind and concentrated on the brooding man beside him.

"What's this got to do with Williams? I don't understand why we're at a hospital." An unpleasant thought occurred to James and he panicked. He came to an abrupt halt, frozen in place just outside the front entrance to the hospital and grabbed Bram's arm, stopping him, as well. "Are you sick? Bram?" His voice was thick with fear. "Are you okay?"

The dark, brooding mood surrounding Bram faded back. His grim expression dissolved, replaced by gentle surprise. He laid a hand over James' where its white knuckled grip held his arm, a pleased, crooked smile on his lips. "Just relax, Jamie. I'm fine." He let the smile spread to his eyes. "But thanks for letting me know you care."

"I *do* care, Bram." Tears leapt to James' eyes again and he blinked furiously to push them back. "More than I probably should, more than I ever have for anyone else." He stepped back and pulled his hand out from under Bram's. "I just need -- I need to be sure."

Bram stared at James, studying him until the other man squirmed. After a moment, he turned on his heel and started walking again. "Then let's go." He headed into the hospital and down the hall to a row of elevators.

James followed closely behind, noticing once again how people responded to Bram. Nurses and technicians greeted Bram by name, several expressing surprise at seeing him again so soon. James was beginning to regret allowing his own insecurities to threaten their relationship.

They took an elevator to the fourth floor and stepped out into the long, gleaming corridor painted a cheerful spring green. As they walked, James distractedly noticed each room was unusually spacious with only one bed in each of them. One had a complex circular frame in the middle of the room in place of a bed.

"I've never heard of this place. What kind of hospital is it?"

Never breaking his stride, Bram talked over his shoulder forcing James to hurry to catch up. "Private rehab, just like the sign out front said." Halfway down the corridor, Bram stopped in front room 414's closed door and turned to face James.

"I'd planned on this happening later on, after I knew if we were going to make a go of this thing," he gestured between them with one hand, "this relationship." Bram rested his hand on James' shoulder and fingered the curls at the base of James' neck. "But apparently, we need to iron out this 'trust issue' first or we're not going to make it past today." His fingers curled around James' neck and gently squeezed, a soft yearning light in his eyes. "And I really want to get *us* past today, Jamie. Together."

An intense, smoldering look came into Bram's face revealing the possessive, predatory desire, lust and need he felt for James.

James felt his chest tighten and his mouth go dry. "I want that too." He returned the heated stare and leaned into Bram's personal space, savoring the scent of sweat and leather clinging to the big man's work clothes. "More than anything, Bram. I do."

Despite the awkwardness of the present situation,

James was flattered and more than little turned on by the man's evident passion. He searched Bram's face for some trace of deception, but found himself pushed close to tears instead. All he could see was genuine love touched with an underlying sadness. James couldn't be sure whether he was the cause of Bram's unhappiness or if it was what was behind the door that was affecting him. He reached up and gripped Bram's forearm and squeezed, returning the intimate, affectionate touch.

Bram's gaze darted over James' eyes, cheekbones and down to his mouth before locking back on his eyes. "Okay then."

Bram backed up and pushed open the door to 414 with his hip, slowly drawing James into the room. His deep voice was suddenly soft and low, pitched for a sleeping child's ears. "Jamie, I'd like you to meet Isabel."

Bram slid his arm around James, tucking him in close to his side. James wasn't sure if it was to keep him from running out or to partially shield him from the sight on the bed.

It was a normal hospital bed, nondescript, made of gray metal and chrome. The siderails were raised on both sides and pale blue cotton fabric over foam padding covered their hard metal bars. On the right side of the bed, a rectangular machine laced with a number of thick cords and wires whooshed and hummed. It pumped heated air down corrugated plastic tubing that ran from the machine and over the rails until it ended at a tube in a hole in the throat of the woman curled up on the bed.

Isabel lay on her right side, arms and legs bent, her ghastly pale, thin limbs cushioned and separated by various blankets and pillows. One thinning, lackluster braid of tarnished gold flowed from her head and down her back, the color the same honey blond as Bram's gleaming hair.

James' gaze was drawn to Isabel's face. Burnt, twisted scars mutilated her entire left side, including her neck. The burn marks trailed down her shoulders and chest to disappear under the hospital gown in an angry swirl of bluish-purple and deep red flesh.

What James could see of the right side of Isabel's face showed the remnants of what was once an attractive young woman. Unable to stop a shudder from racing down his spine, James flinched. He jerked his gaze up to Bram's face horrified he might have offended the man by his unguarded reaction.

Bram ran a hand soothingly down his arm and pulled him closer. "It's okay, Jamie. I know seeing her the first time is a shock. Took awhile before I stopped staring, too." Bram shrugged his shoulders. "Now, I barely notice."

"Jesus, Bram." Suddenly, James thought the situation had just gotten much worse. Who was this woman? What if Bram had brought him here to make a confession? Was Bram bisexual? Was this a past lover, a wife even? Not wanting to know, but desperately needing the answer, James bit his lower lip and tried not to let his voice show how rattled he was. "Who is she?"

"My older sister. My only sister." Taking a deep breath, Bram released James and pulled a chair up to the bedside. He gently picked up Isabel's scarred, misshapen left hand and just held it. He ignored the busy sounds from out in the corridor and the hum and occasional chirping from the machines running to and from his sister's thin body, momentarily lost in his own world of sadness and memories.

A concerned, female voice suddenly cut through

the thick air, startling both men. "Mr. Lord? Bram? Is everything all right?"

Hand resting on Bram's shoulder to comfort him, James jerked around to see a thirty-something woman dressed in pale blue scrubs hovering at the doorway. Bram looked up and gave her a thin smile. James watched as Bram's natural charm cast its spell and the woman's frown transformed into an attractive smile.

"Megan told me you were back again." She walked farther into the room. "We're used to you visiting on Sundays and now you've been here two weekdays in a row."

The nurse looked James over thoroughly, unspoken questions in her eyes, and a slight frown between her brows. "And you brought company. That's a first." Puzzled, she turned back to Bram. "I thought maybe something was wrong."

Shaking his head, Bram winked at the woman in greeting. "Hi, Jill. No, nothing's wrong." He reached up and clasped James' hand still on his shoulder. "I had someone important I wanted to introduce to Isabel."

Bram stood up, drawing James around with him as he turned toward Jill. He slung his arm around James and presented him with a shy smile of affection on his face. "This is James." He looked into James' upturned, surprised face and squeezed his neck playfully. His voiced sank an octave lower and his eyes grew serious. "We're seeing each other." Seeing a smug, knowing grin tug at the corners of the woman's lips, he added, "and yes, he's the reason I didn't get here Sunday."

James blushed and shrugged out of the borrowed over-sized shirt to face the woman.

Laughing behind one chapped hand, Jill extended

her arm and shook James' hand while still talking to Bram. "I'm glad to hear it. You deserve a personal life. You know what they say about 'all work and no play'." She winked at Bram. "But I don't think you'll have that problem with a cutie like him around."

Rolling his eyes, Bram colored a shade darker under his tan and glared at her. "Jamie, this evil woman is Nurse Jill. Jill's been taking care of Isabel ever since she came here. She's great. She knows us both pretty well."

Jill shrugged off the compliment. "Nice to meet you James. I am great," she quipped, "mostly because I know when I'm not needed."

She moved back toward the doorway. "If everything is fine, I'll go tell the rest of the staff. They were concerned at seeing you two days in row and off schedule."

She raised her eyebrows and looked James up and down again. "I'll let them know it's a good change for you, Bram. Bye, James." She wiggled her fingers in the air and hurried out the door.

Bram resumed his seat and cautiously took Isabel's hand again. "You have to be careful not to touch her too much or it sets off seizures. Too much stimulation."

James moved to stand beside him, dropping his voice to just above a whisper. "What happened to her?"

It took a moment before Bram answered. "Car accident, ten years ago. A jilted boyfriend named Gram Watts, had been bothering her after they broke up."

Bram clenched and unclenched his fists as he pulled up the memories. "Just calling her at first then stopping by the office where she worked. Isabel was a CPA with White and White." Bram reached out and stroked his fingertips gently over the strands of golden hair by her temple. "She was a real whiz with numbers." He smiled his lopsided grin. "I used to tease her about being half calculator."

The smile faded from his lips. "But that's all gone now." He pulled back and hunched his shoulders, bracing his elbows on his knees. "After they broke up, Isabel refused to talk to Watts, but he kept calling her. Then he started waiting for her after work, just sitting in his car in the street, watching her."

"Sounds like a real nutcase."

Bram nodded. "He was. I was twenty-four, just finishing up my last year at college. Dad was worried about the whole thing, so he had me drive her home after work every night for awhile. Then Watts up and disappeared."

"I can understand that." James raked his gaze over Bram's impressively large, muscular form. "You'd have that effect on most people, caveman." His tone was warm and affectionate. He rubbed a comforting hand in circles over Bram's back.

"Yeah, so they tell me." Bram sounded weary. He stood up, pressed his lips to James' temple and inhaled, nuzzling his face into the dark curls.

Pulling back, he looked at his sister, the usual spark of vibrancy in his eyes muted by a deep sadness. "Nobody saw him for weeks after that. Isabel was tired of the whole thing and insisted on driving herself again. Mom and Dad had mixed feelings about it, but Isabel could always get her own way."

Bram let out a long, deep sigh and stared at the floor. "I was twenty-four. I had things I wanted to do, places I want to be, and they didn't include playing bodyguard to my big sister all the time. I was happy to have the responsibility lifted off my shoulders."

He sniffled and swallowed hard. "A week later, Gram ran her off the road. She hit a concrete bridge abutment. The car caught fire. It's a miracle she lived at all. Gram hit the same wall. He got the best end of the deal. He died." He glanced at his sister and balled up his fist rapping it against the metal of the siderail. "That was ten years ago."

James looked at the curled, bent woman on the bed in horror. "She's been like this all that time?"

"Pretty much. Doctors tell me she's brain dead. If they shut off the ventilator," he gestured half-heartedly at the humming machine, "and stop the tube feedings," he tilted his head toward a bag of beige fluid hanging from another machine, "she'll die. And they are willing to do it. But *I* have to be the one to say yes."

James thought about Bram's dominating, over-inflated sense of protectiveness and responsibility. He studied the machines surrounding the bed and the frail, shadow of a woman that was all that remained of Bram's family. "But you haven't," he said softly.

Bram looked James in the eye and heaved a huge, trembling sigh. "I know I wasn't responsible for her dying the first time. My head knows it," Bram touched his temple, frustration obvious in his every move, "believes it and understands it, but my heart," he tapped his chest over his left side, "my heart won't let me make her die a second time. I can't do it."

Bram stood as still as a marble statute, tense and rigid, every muscle tightly knotted, fists clenched and knuckles whitened.

"So now you know, Jamie. This is where I was Monday for lunch." Bram shook his head and snorted softly. "I never went to see Williams. After this," he tilted his head toward Isabel's emaciated, lifeless shell, "it's hard to step back, but I know you need to handle him on your own. And I'd never be far away if you needed me. Even now, if you still want to end our relationship, I'll be there if you need me."

James felt every doubt about Bram melted away. He felt his insecurities rising up, leaving him lost and lonely. He suddenly knew there was only one person who could fill the empty part in his life. He was rocked with the realization he was really and truly in love with this man.

Launching himself at Bram, James wrapped his arms around the big man's neck and held on tight. "I'm sorry. I'm so sorry, Bram. I should have trusted you. I'm sorry." He felt the heat of tears collect against his skin and run down into his collar. Hot, hitched gasps burned their way out of his throat and chest.

Bram stroked a hand through James' curls, voice hoarse and whispery. "It's okay, baby. I love you, Jamie. It's all right." Bram tightened his hold. "I got you."

The lonely ache in James' chest dulled and faded to a tiny kernel of guilt-encrusted anxiety. He pushed his last nagging concern about their relationship to the back of his mind then rested his forehead against Bram's furrowed brow and whispered, "You've got me all right, caveman. You've got me good. I love you, too."

They pulled apart far enough to seal their lips together in a gentle but thorough kiss. Bram drew back first and began to rain a series of light kisses over James' face, covering his eyelids, temples, cheeks and chin before returning to James' open and panting mouth. After a long and heated exploration of each other's mouths, Bram framed James' face in his hands and turned gentle eyes on him.

"Come home with me, Jamie. Stay the night. I think I could use some company tonight." Running a hand down James' side and over his backside, Bram cupped the firm cheek and teased the sensitive underside, raking his nails along the fabric of James' thin dress pants.

Squirming, but not pulling away, James let out a shaky breath through pursed lips and gave Bram a doubtful look. "Just sleeping? It's been kind of a rough week."

The big man rolled his forehead against James' brow and chuckled then licked James' pouting lower lip. "If that's what you want, baby. All you need to do is ask."

Pulling free of the enticing embrace, James glanced at the silent bed then grabbing Bram's hand led him toward the door. "Say goodbye, then let's see what happens. Maybe I'm not as tired as I think I am." James left the room, closing the door behind him.

Placing a gentle kiss to Isabel's hair, Bram quietly stepped away from the bed. Glancing at the closed door, he pulled his cell phone from his pocket and hit a pre-set number. He kept one eye on the door as he waited until a gruff voice answered.

"Hey. It's me. I'm not coming back this afternoon. Do me a favor and tell Mitch he has the night off." Bram glanced guiltily at the door again. "No, he'll be with me tonight. Thanks." Bram made to hang up then changed his mind. "I'll be in late in the morning, but I'll be in." Bram listened a moment then chuckled. "You're a pervert, Eddie. Spare me your warped fantasies and get back to work." Flipping it closed, he pocketed the phone and hurried out of the room to his waiting lover.

Chapter Eleven

Bram convinced James to cut his workday shorter than usual. Tired and feeling a disquieting, but persistent need to remain close to Bram, James didn't resist.

Filling the drive to his house with tales from his childhood, Bram gave James a glimpse of what had been his close-knit, happy family. Bram's parents had been accepting of both their children's lives and choices, proud of the adults they had grown-up to be. James was envious.

James suggested take-out food, but Bram insisted on cooking. Dinner was a leisurely meal made together in the warmth of Bram's comfortable, well-appointed kitchen and eaten side-by-side at the island counter. James had agreed to play assistant to Bram's head cook and he had enjoyed it. He enjoyed watching Bram work, covertly admiring his thickly muscled, physical grace and economy of movement. James thought it was like seeing a well-orchestrated ballet.

The sight of the man's firm buttocks under tight, faded jeans as he shifted between stove and countertop while he cooked made James' groin tighten in response. He practically itched with the need to make contact with the man, taking every opportunity he could to brush against Bram while he helped prepare the meal.

They were lingering over the last of the brazed swordfish steak and steamed vegetables when Bram sat back in his chair and sighed, a weary but contented sound. He rolled his head and hunched his shoulders, stretching neck muscles and popping vertebrae. Seeing his opening to make more intimate contact with his lover, James immediately left his chair to stand behind the big man.

"Here, let me see if I can help." Rubbing his fingers and palms into the tight knots of muscle in Bram's neck and shoulders, James stood close enough his stomach touched Bram.

"God, that feels good, Jamie." Bram groaned and dropped his head forward, arching into the heavy caress.

Leaning down, James murmured next to Bram's ear, letting his lips ghost over the sensitive shell as he talked. "Why don't we take this upstairs? I could do a better job if you were stretched out on the bed." He nuzzled the side of Bram's chiseled jaw line and nipped at the soft skin underneath before adding a breathy, "And naked."

The continuous, low moan of pleasure rumbling in Bram's chest mutated into a deep, sexy growl of anticipation and agreement. "I like the sound of that."

Rising up off the stool, Bram twisted around to take James into his arms, capturing his mouth in a heated, prolonged kiss that set both of their libidos soaring.

Walking backwards, Bram dragged James out of the kitchen, down the hallway and up the stairs. Neither of them surfaced for more than a quick breath before diving back down to ravage each other's mouth. Bram held his own in the exchange, but this time James was definitely the more aggressive.

After wrongly accusing Bram of betraying his trust then meeting Isabel and coming to understand more about Bram's protective nature, James felt a deep need to comfort and please Bram. He wanted to apologize with more than just words. He wanted to apologize with love.

Once they made it to the bedroom, James began

undressing his lover, setting a slow, gentle and seductive pace. "Let me do this." He leaned against Bram's chest, unbuttoning the work shirt as he talked, voice low and promising. "You've had a rough day," he ran a hand down through the mat of chest hair he had just exposed, "because of me." He gently lapped at each dusky nipple once and worked the shirt down and off Bram's arms. "Let me help work out some of the tension."

There was an immediate increase in Bram's breathing. Large hands came up to frame James' face and Bram pulled him up for another searing kiss before releasing him.

"I'm all yours, baby. Anything you want, you just ask." Bram dropped his arms to his sides and waited for James' next move.

Feeling empowered, James' own breathing started to come in short little puffs. He slowly dropped to his knees in front of Bram and wordlessly reached for his work boots. Bram assisted with their removal without comment, his gaze locked on James the entire time. Socks were next and James used the opportunity to briefly massage Bram's arches and ankles before reaching higher.

Riveting his sultry, promising gaze to Bram's heated stare, James took his time unbuckling Bram's leather belt. He worked the snap and the pants zipper open, making sure his hands lingered in a heavy touch over the bulge beneath them. Easing the fabric over Bram's tapered, solid hips, he helped the big man step out of them pulling underwear off along with the jeans. James sat back on his heels and enjoyed the view of his naked, buff lover.

Slowly rising to a stand, James took Bram's hand and led him to the already turned down bed. He moved behind Bram and kneaded playfully at his low back, shoving him forward with his fingertips. "Lay down on your stomach and try to relax."

Following James' orders without comment, Bram stretched out on the bed face down. In the center of the massive bed, Bram settled in, splaying his legs in a V and extending his arms high and wide to touch the headboard, sending several pillows tumbling to the floor in their wake. Various tan lines marked his Adonis-like frame, outlining different shirt sleeve lengths and giving James an idea how brief Bram's swimsuit was.

Bram arched his back, flexing his body like a cat, working the muscle groups down his impressive body until even his toes spread and stretched, then his entire frame collapsed onto the mattress, waiting. Bram's face was turned to one side pillowed on nothing but the empty sheets. After a moment, he shifted his weight and raised one knee to make room for his half-hard erection.

The sight of Bram spread-eagle and waiting for him brought a flush to James' entire body and his cock jumped and quivered. Afraid his desire to have sex with Bram would override his desire to pleasure the man unselfishly, James had to turn around and quickly undress in order to maintain control.

He was surprised, but pleased to see a box of wet-ones and several small hand towels had been added to the bedside table since Sunday, along with three bottles of various lotions in an orderly row to one side. A large based candle sat in the middle of the items, like a beacon lighting the way to a path of new pleasures.

James examined the bottles finding one to be lube and the other two massage oils. Delighted, he lit the candle using the small disposable lighter next to it and chose one of the unscented oils.

Naked, half-hard and panting, James climbed onto the bed and knelt beside Bram's waist. He rested one hand in the middle of Bram's back to ground his lover with his touch then ran his hand up the valley of Bram's spine from the crease of his firm buttocks to the base of his spine. Bram responded with a low moan and arched into the light touch.

"Hang in there, caveman. I'm just getting started. Keep your hands down, okay?" He didn't expect an answer and he didn't get one. Bram merely flexed his hands against the sheets.

James rose up and straddled Bram's hips, settling his hot, open crotch over the center of Bram's ass, and letting his sac rest in the warm, hairy divide.

Bram's moan dropped an octave and he spread his legs wider.

Filling his palms with the thick massage oil, James rubbed them together to warm it. Placing both hands at the base of Bram's spine in front of him, James worked his way up the hard flesh, kneading hard against the variety of knots he encountered and massaging the oil deep into the tense muscles and satin smooth skin. While working his hands over and over the hard plains and rippling tissues just to feel the power and strength in the muscle , he was amazed at the silky texture of the man's flawless expanse of flesh.

Bram groaned when James worked the tight knots and moaned again when he caressed the smooth strips of sensitive muscle. His tone alternated between a low growl and soft rumble whenever James stroked over his more sensitive spots. James memorized these as future places to investigate when the massage was over and their playtime had moved onto more serious pursuits.

James worked his way up each of Bram's arms, massaging each palm and finger in turn then worked his way back down Bram's spine. He kneaded and prodded the hard flesh of the man's neck and shoulders until the flesh was hot and pliant under his hands. Bram let a nearly constant hum of approval. James lifted off Bram's ass and slide down between the man's spread legs to his feet. He massaged and stroked, loosening Bram's muscles from his toes up. He paid homage to sensitive arches, around rough heels and strong ankles to knead thickly corded calf muscles and stout, iron hard thighs.

Finally, James moved up between Bram's knees to cup and caress the twin globes of his rounded, taut butt, massaging and stroking the muscular area with firm hands. His thumbs snaked along the deep crease with each pass, invading deeper and deeper until they brushed across the dark, furry opening to Bram's body.

Both men gleamed in the soft fading light of the afternoon. James wore a fine sheen of sweat. The candle began to throw gray shadows around the bed, intensifying the visual effects of the oil on Bram's golden skin.

James' cock was hard and leaking. Sometime during the massaging of his ass, Bram had shifted his growing cock to point down between his spread legs. James could see the dusky head under and extending past Bram's large, tight sac.

James crawled up Bram's back and settled his body over Bram's back. He nuzzled the man's honey blond hair with his whole face, inhaling the rich scent of leather and sweat that was his lover's own. Finding the tip of one earlobe, he mouthed it, sucking and nibbling a moment before panting hot air into the now wet outer shell and whispering a new command.

"Turn over. I want to finish you."

The body under him went from lax and pliant to taut and lithe in a millisecond. Bram turned in one smooth motion, carrying James with him. He turned the smaller man as he spun so they ended up lying chest-to-chest, with James still on top and Bram flat on his back.

Gasping, the sheer power of the man shot through James, riding on a sizzling rail of excitement and sexual energy that ripped down his spine and ignited the embers of fire already smoldering in his groin. Bram was an amazing powerhouse. His strength was raw and primal, contained and governed by the big man's deep sense of moral responsibly and solid sense of right and wrong.

Bright, lustful eyes stared up at James. Bram held him around the waist and the big man slowly dragged James' torso down his own until their cocks nudged each other. James watched Bram's pupils dilate with fierce arousal then mute as tenderness invaded the stare. James' love for Bram rooted itself deeper into his heart at that moment.

"Hang onto that thought, caveman." James panted and reluctantly slid off to kneel between Bram's spreading thighs, trying to ignore what Bram's deep, unhappy growl did to his straining cock. "I'm not done with you yet."

He tore his gaze away from Bram's seductive, hungry stare and reclaimed his fallen bottle of oil. The big man purred and stretched under his freshly oiled hands and watched James' every move from half-lidded, dilated and hungry eyes.

James was delighted to find the massage turned his dirty talking, aggressive, hugely satisfying lover into a sensuous, rippling animal that responded in mostly raw nimal sounds and impressive, lithe, cat-like moves. /ariety was going to be the spice of their lives for a long ime to come.

Starting at the tips of Bram's long toes, James stroked and massaged his way up to the man's hips, ubbing past the swaying cock jutting proudly and nsistently in the air. He worked oil into each bulging high, paying attention to the crease between groin and eg, but never moving onto the thick mound of pubic nuscle over Bram's pelvis. He straddled Bram's thighs, orcing them together then slowly worked his way up the nan's solid lower abdomen to his impressive six-pack abs. ames worked each rib, tracing its curve around the side and coming back on the next higher bone.

Careful to avoid anything but the smallest of contact with their erections, James settled his crotch over Bram's waist and pressed his knees to the man's body, capturing him in their grip. He worked up each arm, adding light kisses to the insides of the elbows and underarms, inhaling the man's scent along the way. Bram had once again turned plaint and James had to work at raising the heavy limbs.

Registering the gradual increases in Bram's breathing by the slightly labored sounds and the rhythm of the chest heaving under his spread legs, James finally felt his own cravings were under control enough to lock stares with Bram again.

The moment their gazes met, Bram's face flushed a deeper shade and his eyes turned almost black. The growl that shook his chest vibrated through James' groin and made his cock jerk and harden until it ached. Bram's lips twisted and he opened his mouth to pant. His nostrils flared and his hips began to buck in tiny, involuntary jerks.

James took his cue and slid off Bram's body before the choice was taken from him. He quickly licked a trail down Bram's chest, abdomen and groin then moved between Bram's legs. Both of his oiled hands latching onto the thick purple cock begging for attention. He rubbed his face over the shaft and head, letting the stiff rod slap his face.

Bram's hands shot to the top of the bed and latched onto the headboard in a white-knuckled grip, chest heaving, nipples turning a dusky rose and peaking into firm nubs atop glistening, hard pads of muscle. The moan was gratifying for James to hear and it increased his desire to please his lover.

Placing one hand at the root of Bram's wide cock and the other directly above it, James squeezed and twisted first one direction and then the other, raining open-mouthed, wet kisses to the leaking tip. Feeling the shaft harden and grow in his hands, James took the head into his mouth and worked his tongue around the sensitive edge. Bram's hips bucked at the contact, forcing James to use his arms to press the big man back down to the mattress.

Adding suction to the tonguing action pulled a long, agonized groan from his lover and James renewed his efforts. He varied his rhythm for several minutes then settled into a firm stroking motion with both hands. Drawing the engorged head in just past his lips, James lapped at the surface with the flat of his tongue, sucking in a rapid pattern of tiny movements that stimulated the underside of the bulb as well as the tip. He felt the shaft thicken and grow impossibly harder just before the muscles under his grip began to pulsate.

Bram let out a roar that sent shivers through James as he pumped threads of thick, salty cum into James' eager mouth.

Looking up from under his lashes as he sucked, James devoured the sight of Bram's oiled body arching and tensing in the throes of a blinding orgasm. Every muscle on Bram's frame bulged and rippled in time to his spurting cock, the convulsing of his gorgeous body like an exotic dance of primal lust. James matched his sucking and swallowing to the beat and rode out the fierce tide of heat and cum.

The heavy wooden headboard thumped against the wall as Bram gave one more explosive growl and emptied the last of his juices onto James' tongue. Licking the final droplets out of the slit, James eased the softening cock out of his mouth and ran his tongue over his lips. Head slightly bowed, he looked up at his gasping lover and slowly crawled up Bram's body, allowing the tip of his cock to graze up Bram's flesh as he moved, to sit on the big man's chest. James' own erection was bobbing tall and proud, eagerly seeking out contact. His voice was raspy and low, husky with need.

"Watch me come for you, Bram. Just for you."

Palming the dusky shaft, James locked his gaze with Bram's still hungry stare and began jerking off, playing to a private audience of one. James grunted and moaned, knowing it wouldn't take much to push him over the edge. His eyes slid partly shut at the sharp sensations his over-stimulated cock was experiencing and he barely registered when Bram's arms moved down and warm hands slid up his thighs.

"Come here, baby."

A firm tugging on his hips forced James to open

his eyes again. Bram had pulled a pillow under his head and it made the candlelight sparkle in the blue pools of his eyes. James felt like the man's gaze was pulling him forward. He shook his head and continued to work his aching cock, determined to make this time all for Bram.

"No hands, remember? Want this to be just for you." James panted and squirmed, increasing his rhythm, thumbing the tip of his cock to bring himself off faster.

"I said, *come here*!" A raw, guttural sound rumbled out of Bram's throat and James was yanked forward. His chest collided with the headboard and he had to grab onto its top edge to keep his face from making contact with the carved wooden surface. His knees landed on either side of Bram's head, his hips locked in a bruising grip that promised to leave finger marks for days to come.

Before James could utter a sound in protest, Bram swallowed down his cock, deep throating him in one swift action that took James' stuttered breath away. James pressed his face into the headboard and cried out as Bram pressed the flat surface of his hot, wet tongue against the underside of his near to bursting cock and wiggled the slippery muscle. The strong, blunt fingers on his flanks rubbed deep into his flesh and James felt his pelvis become more congested as blood pounded into his lower regions.

Taking a deep breath, James was shocked into holding it when Bram swallowed again, milking the length of his rod with tight throat muscles.

Looking down, James saw Bram's face flush with his groin and he grew lightheaded with lust. Bram's lips massaged the base of James' cock, taking him in all the way until they were buried in the sparse hair surrounding it. Bram added a twist of his neck and suction, and the breath James had been holding escaped as a scream. He exploded down the big man's throat, pulsing and pounding against the immobilizing hold on his hips. James' awareness faded in and out as the last of his cum was swallowed .

James felt his pliant body gently manhandled to a prone position and a familiar scent invaded his mind. Eyes closed, he nuzzled the skin beneath him and felt a prickly five o'clock shadow rasp against his cheek. Strong hands soothed over his back and sides. Eventually, the sensation of a sheet floated down over his back and he slowly raised his head to meet Bram's amused, content expression.

"Hey, baby. Nice massage. You can work the tension out of me anytime you want." Bram's lopsided smile and rugged good looks were especially nice by candlelight.

James' voice was weak and raspy. "You don't play fair. I said no hands." He dropped his head and buried his face in Bram's hair.

Bram chuckled and pulled James closer, kissing his forehead lightly. "All's fair in love and war, baby. And this is definitely love."

Grunting a monosyllable that could have been either agreement or argument, James let exhaustion take hold and he drifted off, enjoying the warmth and closeness of his lover's embrace, knowing the deeply rooted feeling of completion he had was more than just a physical bond now.

Chapter Twelve

The morning sunlight filtered through James' office window and reflected off the sleek golden statue sitting on the middle of his desk, grabbing James' attention.

It was a gift, a token of affection from Bram, found on his trip to Chicago. It depicted a small, lean cheetah intertwined with a large, thick-muscled lion, illustrating a scene from an ancient Chinese myth representing two differing, but compatible, personalities in male intimates.

Bram had reassured James the cheetah fit his personality perfectly, with his own dominant strengths embodied by the lion.

James had spent the afternoon lingering over memories of sleeping curled comfortably next to Bram and gazing at the small statue. He was lost in thought again when his phone buzzed, making him jump. Flustered, he stumbled over his greeting and hurriedly acknowledged his boss's secretary's request to go to Dunn's office.

It took him exactly two minutes to arrive at Dunn's door, suit coat on and tie straight. He ran a hand through his unruly curls, wishing he had packed a bag to leave at Bram's before this so he would have the kind of hair care products his fine curls responded to best. Bram didn't appear to use baby shampoo and James had been too embarrassed to ask. He'd settled for flyaway hair instead.

On his arrival, Dunn's secretary smiled and nodded at the partially open door, never breaking away rom her phone conversation. James took the cue and entered.

Placing a framed picture he had been looking at down on his desktop, Dunn rose from behind his gleaming mahogany desk. He had a smile on his face and his hand out stretched in greeting.

"Good morning, James." Dunn shook James' hand hen motioned toward one of two chairs in front of his desk. "Please, sit down."

"Thank you, Mr. Dunn." James sat and was surprised when Dunn took the chair next to him instead of returning to the seat behind his desk.

Philip Dunn, a tall, graying, trim figured man in his mid-fifties, was one of the original founders of Dunn & Piper. His lifelong friend and partner, Michael Piper, had passed away ten years ago. Dunn, along with the political and financial influence his wife had, managed to continue nurturing the small company into one of the city's most successful architectural firms.

James knew it was a credit to his talent to be part of the firm. His job was very important to him. Before Bram, it was all he had.

Fidgeting slightly, James resettled on the chair and looked expectantly at his boss.

Dunn draped an arm casually over the arm of the chair and relaxed back into the cushions. "I'm sure you probably know why I called you in here, James."

Eyes wide, James darted his gaze around the room looking for a clue for the summons. Seeing nothing except paperwork and a recent picture of Dunn with a much older woman, he looked back at his boss and shook his head.

"Ah, no sir. I don't." James bit at his lower lip then

released it. "Everything is coming along as well as can be expected on the Tork project, considering we've only had it two days." His eyes widened even more. "Unless there's a problem I'm not aware of, sir."

Dunn reached out and patted James' arm comfortingly. "No, no. It's nothing like that, James. It's more of a personal matter." Dunn sat back and gave James a small smile. "The dinner party Friday night. I still haven't heard back from you about whether or not you'll be bringing a friend." Dunn's smile grew fond. "My wife is quite a stickler about proper seating and making sure couples are paired off in compatible groups. She won't give me a moments peace until she knows if you're bringing someone."

James sucked in his bottom lip and chewed on the corner of it. He dropped his gaze and studied the knot of Dunn's tie for a moment.

"There's no shame in coming alone, James, but my sources tell me you're seeing someone." Dunn chuckled at the startled look on James' face as his head popped up to look Dunn in the eye. "And pretty heavily, too. Am I right?"

Thinking back, James remembered seeing one of the secretaries outside when Bram picked him up the other evening. Licking his dry lips, James cleared his throat and answered. "Yes, sir. I am."

"Someone special?"

James just nodded, unable to find the words to keep this conversation from going somewhere he wasn't prepared to go with his boss just yet. "Special enough to introduce to your boss and co-workers?"

Swallowing past the growing lump of fear in his throat, James nodded again. "I'd like to, yes." He shifted nervously in his chair and looked at Dunn. "But it's not that easy. At least, not for me."

Mindless of the wrinkles and creases he was putting in the finely tailored trousers, Dunn leaned forward in his chair and rested his elbows on his knees, "James. I try to keep my company a close-knit organization. There is room in it for everyone who is willing to work hard and has a high set of standards for themselves. I think you fall into that definition. You're a talented, truly gifted young architect and I know you'll do great things for the company."

"Thank you, sir."

"No thanks needed, James. It's true. More importantly, I want to get to know you on a deeper level than just employee to employer. I like to think of all my architects as an extended part of my family."

Dunn's gaze flickered to the desk and back to James' earnest, surprised face. "My wife and I were never blessed with children. A psychiatrist would probably tell you I'm making up for that by trying to adopt my staff, but I don't care. The people here are the biggest part of my life and I like them involved in it on more than a business level, if they want. It's always a matter of personal choice, James."

James thought the expression in Dunn's eyes looked like he was trying to convey a deeper meaning to James.

"I respect people, their lifestyles and their choices."

"There is someone I want to be there with me." James felt embarrassed and at a loss for words. He had no idea how Dunn felt about gays and now wasn't the time he would have picked to find out. He had enough on his mind sorting out his feelings for Bram without worrying about his job as well. James took a deep breath and turned to face Dunn.

"My choice might cause some . . . discomfort for your other guests. I don't want to create an unpleasant situation, for me, my date or you and your wife."

"Unless you show up with the one of the other architect's wives, I doubt you could ruffle many feathers, James."

Resigned, James sighed and dropped his gaze to absently study the objects on Dunn's desk. "All the same, Mr. Dunn, it might be best if I just worked late Friday night."

Snorting an objection, Dunn rose from his chair. "Nonsense. You'll do nothing of the sort. I'll expect you and your date at six o'clock sharp for cocktails and gossip." Patting James on the shoulder, he walked around his desk.

Taking Dunn's movement as a cue for dismissal, James stood and made to leave. "Thanks all the same, sir. I think it'd be best if we wait until next time."

James turned, but Dunn's voice, tougher and angrier than James would have believed, stopped him in his tracks.

"Do you know what this is?"

Turning around, James shifted his gaze between Dunn's stern face and the framed photograph in his outstretched hand. It was the picture from his desk. James looked at it closer and shrugged.

"It's a photograph of you and a lovely older woman." Judging the woman to be Dunn's senior by at least twenty years, James hazarded a guess. "Your mother?"

Some of the anger drained from Dunn's

expression, but it still remained stern. "That's the logical conclusion and it's what most people think."

Dunn ran his fingertips over the glass, a gentle fondness in his tone and gesture. "But they're wrong. It's a picture of me and my wife, Lenore."

"Oh." Blinking back his surprise, James blushed when Dunn chuckled at his reaction.

"Most people have a lot more to say than that. Still a beautiful woman, Lenore is twenty three years older than I am." Dunn set the frame down. "We made a dashing couple back when I was twenty-five and just starting out in business. She was the ex-wife of one of my father's partners and sharp businesswoman in her own right. I fell for her the moment we met. But there were a lot of taboos against marrying an older woman back then, let alone a divorcee to boot."

His eyes reflected a lot of old pain and unpleasant memories. "We met a lot of resistance to our being a couple, but we never let it stop us from loving each other. Not in thirty years."

Dunn looked James in the eye, a distinctly paternal expression on his handsome, slightly wrinkled-at-the-corners face. "You see, James, I know a little about making choices for love that don't fit the traditional mold the rest of society would like to jam us into."

Swallowing hard, James concentrated on slowing down his suddenly irregular breathing. Silent, he stared at Dunn, trying to be sure he was hearing the acceptance and understanding he thought he was hearing.

Dunn leaned forward and lowered his voice, a note of amusement in the light tone. "Do you really think I'm not aware of the fact that if you brought a date you were serious about to the party that it would be a man?"

Blushing again, James lowered his gaze to the floor and shrugged. "I-I didn't know you knew. And I didn't know how you would feel about it." He looked back up and squared his shoulders. "It's not a secret. I mean, my being gay. I just don't make an issue out of it."

"I'm not going to either. I'm also not going to let it be the reason you continue to keep your distance from people here."

James head jerked up and bit his lip, staring wide-eyed at his boss.

"Yes, James, I know what you've been doing. Your co-workers have all commented on how kind, sweet natured, enormously talented and intelligent you are. They also mention how isolated and distant you keep yourself."

Dunn couldn't stop the smile that tugged at his lips. "At least until this last week. The secretaries are all a buzz about the 'handsome hunk of muscle', as they called him, who picked you up from work twice this week."

"Oh, God." James groaned and buried his face in his hands.

Dunn chuckled and lowered his voice to a whisper, tilting his head towards the outer office that housed his secretary. "Macy made a point to mention she even saw him drop you off this morning at an ungodly hour."

Brow furrowed, Dunn glanced at the closed door. "That woman must get here before the sun comes up. No wonder she has everything done before I get here." Dunn humphfed. "Must be why I pay her so much."

"I'm sorry, Mr. Dunn. I never expected my personal life to be the subject of gossip. I-I don't know what to say."

"You don't have to say anything. I know from personal experience, you can't be happy in your work if you're not happy in your life. I want happy people working for me, James."

A closeted part of James peeked out from the dark hole where he normally kept it hidden. Once it stepped into the bright light of acceptance, it faded away. James was left with a surprising revelation in its place.

"Thank you, Mr. Dunn." James grimaced and glanced at the secretary's door. "Not the gossip part, but the understanding. Worrying about things -- my job, how people here would react in a social setting -- has been keeping me from doing something I really need to do."

He reached out and shook Dunn's hand again, this time with a lot more enthusiasm. "I hope you don't mind, but I have to leave right now. I have someone I need to ask to dinner." Turning on his heel, James hurried out the door.

Dunn called out after him. "I'll tell Lenore to make that two by your name. Good luck, James." He chuckled to himself and picked up the picture again. "Should be quite an evening."

***

James called his lover as he left the office and insisted Bram meet him. James was already waiting for him on the front porch when Bram arrived.

Bram strode up the sidewalk outside his house, a concerned frown marring his face. He was wearing a dress shirt and slacks, a short leather coat over the open neck shirt. His customary cowboy boots pounded a rhythmic staccato on the concrete walk.

"Jamie? What's the problem? Are you alright?" Grabbing James by both arms, Bram swung the smaller man around and looked him over from head to toe, scrutinizing every visible inch.

A reckless expression on his face, James decided not to waste time or words. He took hold of Bram's jacket and yanked him through the front door as soon as Bram opened it. "I need to talk with you and I couldn't do it out there."

"Slow down and tell me what's going on." Confused, Bram closed the door and turned to watch James frantically pacing across the open entryway.

The younger man was mumbling to himself, gesturing in the air with his hands. When his familiar nervous habit of biting on his lower lip threatened to draw blood, Bram gently took hold of James' shoulder as he passed in front of him and brought the pacing to a halt.

"Stop and talk to me, Jamie." Bram turned James around so they were face-to-face and bent down to look into his eyes. "You sounded like this was pretty important on the phone. I canceled two meetings to be here. Now stop trying to chew your lip off and talk to me."

Taking a deep breath, James nodded and released his abused lip. "Remember when I said I couldn't see you this Friday night? That I had work plans?" Bram nodded and opened his mouth to answer, but James cut him off. "I lied."

Never letting go of his hold on James' shoulders, Bram's frown deepened as James cut off his attempt at comment again.

"Not really *lied* lied, but it wasn't the complete truth, either." Bram's expression struggled to remain neutral in the face of James' conflicting explanation. "It's a dinner party. At my boss's house, Mr. Dunn's." James could see the confusion in Bram's face and he tried to clarify the situation. "And I'm supposed to bring a date, which would be you," James erratically flicked a hand back and forth between them, "but I was afraid to. Afraid to be me in front of the people I work with. Afraid to make a commitment." James twisted his fingers into Bram's shirtfront and held on, a panicked expression of uncertainty on his face. "Commitment to you."

"I see." The disappointment was clear in Bram's low, discouraged tone. Bram moved to turn away, but the fingers in his shirt held on tighter, keeping him in place.

"No, no you don't see, Bram. I didn't either, at first, but now I do."

"What do you see, Jamie? Tell me. Because I can't live my life lying to people, pretending not to be something I am." Bram pulled James up closer to his chest and stared down into James' uneasy face. "Not even for you, Jamie. It'd kill off part of me and then neither one of us would be able to stand me."

"I don't want you to change. I love the way you are. I want to be *like* you. That's what I'm trying to tell you." James loosened his fingers from Bram's shirt to grab hold of one of the man's thick wrists, pulling him toward the staircase. "Come here. I need to explain a few things."

Bram allowed James to tug him along and they sat down side-by-side on the same step. James threaded his fingers through Bram's and rested their intertwined hands on his knees. "I need to tell you about my family." He covered the back of Bram's hand with his other palm and tightened his grip, holding on like this was his only anchor in the rough seas he was about to navigate. The responding grip around his hand gave James enough reassurance to continue.

"I was wondering about them." Bram moved his leg close until it rubbed along side James' thigh.

Savoring the warmth and intimate contact, James relaxed a bit. "You shouldn't." He studied the thick, callused hand in his. His voice trembled. "You won't like them. They're not like yours were. Not by a long shot."

"That bad?"

"Yeah. That bad." James took a deep breath and slowly let it out. "I have three sisters, all older than me, Julie, Jane, and Jennifer. I'm three years younger than Jen."

James stared off into space, and watched the dust molecules dance in the fading afternoon light. "Dad works in a manufacturing plant, on the assembly line. Mom stays home. Both Jane and Jennifer are married. They live close to my parents. Julie's a lawyer, still single, with a mind of her own." He gave Bram a weak smile and gnawed at his lower lip. "You'll like Julie. She's the only one that'll talk to me."

"What do you mean, Jamie? If they're still alive, why don't you talk?"

"When I was a senior in college, all three of my sisters came up to visit me at my dorm, to surprise me for my birthday. My roommate was a real jerk. He thought it would be funny to unlock our door and let my sisters into our dorm room to wait for me. Except he knew I was in the room with my boyfriend, in bed, celebrating my birthday. Janie and Jen ran from the room practically screaming. Julie left to go after them, but not before she belted my roommate."

"I'm sorry that happened to you. I can't imagine how you felt."

"It gets better. I went home that weekend. Janie

wouldn't even talk to me and Jen kept making crude remarks until she finally came right out and told my parents about me and my boyfriend. My dad exploded. He and I had a huge fight that ended when he punched me out. I left and I've never gone back. Dad stopped helping pay for school after that. I got a job, several jobs in fact, and finished my senior year."

James sighed and rubbed at his forehead. "Julie came for graduation and she calls about once a month. She says mom and dad still love me, but . . .," James' voice hitched and he wiped at his eyes under the guise of pushing his hair off his face, "the last time I saw my mom, she looked like she was going to cry for the rest of her life."

Hooking an arm gently around James' hunched shoulders, Bram's voice was soft and understanding. "No wonder you have a little problem trusting people."

"Little?" James snorted and closed his eyes. "I've never felt so betrayed in my life. It seemed everyone betrayed me, first my roommate, then Jen and my own parents. Mom never said a word when dad was throwing me out." A tear broke loose and slid down his cheek, hastily brushed away with nervous fingers. "But I can't change who I am." He looked up at Bram, eyes full of hope and fear. "I knew it then and I know it now."

"I'm glad about that." Bram briefly squeezed James.

"Don't get me wrong. It's still hard to think about being as open as you are, but I'm willing to work on it. If you'll help me, be patient with me." James turned into the embrace and wrapped his arms around Bram's waist. "I really want this to work between us, Bram. I know it's not an excuse for not telling you the truth about the dinner or accusing you of seeing Williams, but it's an explanation."

James whispered so softly Bram had to strain to hear it. "You understand so much about me already, what I need, instinctively, I wanted you understand about this, too. I've never confessed this to anyone else, ever."

Pulling James closer, Bram rested his chin on James' curly head and took a deep breath. "While we're making confessions here, I have one to tell you."

James stiffened a little in Bram's arms, prepared to hear the worst. It had been too much to expect the other man to accept the distrust and hesitancy. Bram had been nothing but assured and giving from the start. James wasn't surprised Bram wasn't willing to settle for an uncertain lover. Bram deserved more from a potentially permanent relationship.

James was surprised how much the thought of losing Bram made him tremble and even more surprised when the tremors shook the outside of his body, as well as the inside.

"Hey, Jamie, what the hell is all the shaking about?" The arms around him tightened sharply and Bram ran a soothing hand up and down his back and arm. "My confession isn't all that bad. At least I hope you won't think so."

James couldn't find his voice, the crazy hope in his head that if he didn't ask, Bram wouldn't tell him it was over. James bit his lower lip so hard he drew blood. Unable to see James' face and the trickle of blood, Bram continued.

"It's about Williams." James went rigid again and Bram hurried with his explanation. "I didn't go see him, but I did try and make sure he didn't try anything." Bram sighed and plunged ahead, rubbing and squeezing the ense, lean shoulders under his massive hand. "I know ou didn't want me to get involved but I couldn't leave ou alone there every night with that creep two doors lown."

James wiggled free of the tight embrace and pulled ack far enough to look at Bram's contrite face. Eyebrows urrowed in confusion, he just looked at the other man ntil Bram continued.

"Okay, okay, don't look at me like that. It's no big hing." The exasperation at having to explain himself was lear in his voice, along with a little embarrassment. "I just sked Mitch and a couple of the guys to make sure you ot home safe at night while I was out of town and navailable."

The frown on James' face deepened. "How?"

Bram hesitated then sighed, gripping James' hands n both of his. "They waited at your building after work. Outside. Made sure you got in the door and that the lights ame on in your apartment in a reasonable amount of ime." The guilty look on Bram's face was tempered with letermination. "I wasn't going to leave you on your own o deal with that asshole."

James raised his eyebrows at that, giving Bram a lisbelieving glare.

Bram sputtered and colored slightly. "It was just wo nights! And they never went in the building! Any ime Williams harassed you it was out in the hall. I figured ou were safe if you made it inside your place."

"That's all they did?" James asked suspiciously.

"Mostly." Bram admitted grudgingly. "Mitch nsisted on staying until your lights went out both nights, out that was his decision."

"*Mitch*?" James was incredulous.

"Yeah, Mitch. He thinks you look like one of those tiny poodles. All curls and wide eyes." Bram smiled when a pissed off expression replaced the slightly frightened, uncertain one on James' face. "He says you're little, but you've got sharp tiny teeth and a kick-ass attitude." The frown dissolved a little. "He likes you." Bram ruffled the curls on James' head. "Thinks I should keep you." The playful tousle turned into a gentle, sensual caress. "I agree." Bram's voice dropped an octave and a gentle light came into his eyes.

James felt his mouth fall open in surprised and the trembling of his limbs increased until he was shivering. Licking at the split in his lip, he studied Bram's waiting expectant expression. His voice was low and shook as much as his body did.

"You still want me? After all this shit?"

"What's not to want? You not perfect, Jamie, but neither am I. What do you say we work on our shortcomings together?" Bram pulled James up and around and had him straddle his lap on the stairs.

James settled comfortably onto Bram and folded into a warm, sheltering embrace in the big man's arms. "I should be mad at you about the babysitting thing, but I'm not." He dropped a quick kiss on the end of Bram's chin. "I think it was an outstanding, loving thing to do."

"Good." Bram ducked his head and quirked his eyebrows high for a second, looking sheepish. "I was afraid it was going to piss you off."

"It did." James tried to scowl at his lover, but it came off as lame when a twisted smile tugged at one corner of his mouth. "Or would have," he sighed. "If I'd known about it at the time." He smacked Bram's chest hard with his open palm, but the big man seemed too preoccupied with gazing lovingly down at his feisty lover to notice. "But now it seems just . . . sweet. Kind of makes me feel protected and cared for." James' tone turned wistful. "Haven't felt that in a long time."

The endearingly sexy, lopsided grin spread across Bram's face, but James wasn't falling for it. "But that *doesn't* mean you should do it again, caveman."

Laughing, Bram hugged James closer and slid his hands under James' butt, caressing and massaging the twin globes of flesh as he talked. "Okay. I won't ask Mitch and the guys to sit outside your apartment again. But that doesn't mean I won't be watching out for you. I won't promise to stop doing that, Jamie, so don't ask."

Shifting deeper onto Bram's lap, James pushed against the warm, kneading palms doing interesting things to his backside, encouraging Bram to shift his focus lower to James wide-spread and interested crotch.

"Fine. We make no promises that we know we can't keep." James dipped his head and latched onto Bram's chin, licking and sucking at the cleft in the prickly skin. He felt an immediate surge in the flesh under his ass. He sucked harder and rasped his tongue over the rough surface, teasing the faint shadow of beard and the sensitive skin under it.

"Go with me to the dinner party tomorrow night? I want to introduce my boyfriend to my boss."

The response was instantaneous. Bram softly growled deep in his throat and began nuzzling James' throat with his nose inhaling deeply. "Anything you want, baby, anything." He added teeth and lips, working his way up to James' ear to nibble at the lobe.

Gasping, James began a humping rhythm on Bram's lap, rubbing both their growing erections together.

"Bram?"

The other man continued to nuzzle, lick and suck his way around, over and into every part of James' neck and face he could reach as his murmured, "What, baby?"

James began unfastening both of their pants, hands frantic in their haste.

"You said all I ever have to do is ask and you'll do it?"

Bram's hands joined his and they both grunted when cock met cock. James wrapped both hands around the two rods and savored the feeling of the heated flesh pulsing and growing at his touch.

"Yeah, baby, just ask."

Bram's voice was raw and gritty, pushed out between clamped teeth as he wrapped his hands around James' and added pressure to the liquid movement of James' strokes.

"Do me, caveman, in every room in the house." James had to stop to gain control of his breathing then panted, "Start right here by the front door, here on the stairs." He groaned as Bram bent down to spit on their cocks, swirling his callused thumbs through the thick saliva. "Make me cum." His entire body jerked at the added stimulation. "Mark me in every spot you own."

The answering growl let James know he had been granted his request. Bram slowly nudged James' hands off their cocks and wrapped one of his own massive fists around them, adding more spit and more muscle to the grip.

James moved one hand to Bram's head to bring him in for a passionate kiss and worked his other under their cocks to play with the twin sacs nestled tightly together between his legs. A light tug on Bram's rewarded

James with a gasp and an increase in the stroking.

Suddenly, Bram changed tactics, using both hands to work their cocks, slowly dragging one slicked hand down from crown to root, instantly followed by his other hand doing the same motion, again and again.

James felt like his cock was plowing deeper and deeper into a hot, tight hole of muscular flesh that never stopped. His breathing sped-up and he had to break away from the kiss to gasp in more air.

Bram refused to let James pull away. He latched onto James' neck and nibbled sharply at the skin between shoulder and neck, making sure there would be marks of his claim for several mornings to come.

The saliva disappeared and a heated chaffing began to register with James. He found the slight burn heightened his need and he pumped his hips in rhythm with Bram's strokes. Bram rubbed at the underside of his cock's head.

James was suddenly bathed in hot spurts of thick cum. He looked down to watch Bram explode, the sight of their joined slippery knobs being coated in white cream sending him over the edge. He arched his back and grabbed onto Bram's shoulders, frozen in place on the man's lap while Bram continued to milk the last teaspoon of cum from their bodies. Bright lights sparked behind his clenched eyelids and it felt like electricity shot from his cock, leaving a tingling buzz of lingering excitement in his spine.

Collapsing against his heaving lover, James matched Bram's labored breaths, gasp for gasp. When his breathing was back to something close to normal, James leaned back so he could see Bram. They held each other's gaze for a moment then Bram gently threaded his hands through James' hair and pulled him forward for a blistering, no-holds-barred kiss.

James lost his ability to breathe again. He was reduced to an exhausted puddle of bone and tissue, clinging for support to Bram's solid, rippling body. Bram's mouth and tongue explored every inch of his own, stealing his breath and soothing his damaged heart at the same time.

The sudden thought that he had almost come close to losing this man, this feeling, shot through him and tears welled in his eyes and a spear of ice lanced down his spine making him shiver.

Feeling the tremors rack his lover, Bram broke the kiss. Hands still firmly buried in James' hair, Bram anxiously searched James' face. "What's the matter, baby?" He gently brushed away a single tear trickling down James' cheek.

Smiling despite the tears, James shook his head. "Nothing. Not a thing -- as long as you're with me, I'm good." He dropped a quick kiss to Bram's furrowed brow and grinned. "I'm probably going to suffer brain damage from lack of oxygen though, if you keep on kissing me like that." He slowly leaned in and kissed Bram more thoroughly, lingering over it, savoring the taste of the man.

James whispered into Bram's mouth between kisses. "But I'm willing to risk it." He jerked his head toward the upstairs bedroom. "Why don't we go upstairs and see if we can kill off a few more?"

The lopsided grin of delight widened. Bram grabbed James around the waist and stood up, anchoring James' legs around his hips. He lightly kissed James then turned and started up the steps.

"All you ever have to do is ask, baby."

Chapter Thirteen

Burying his face in the bunched bed cover, James hissed into the fabric mound and fisted the sheets over the mattress tighter. Bent over the low bed, ass high in the air he spread his bare feet wider on the carpet and pushed back against the cock slamming into him from behind. Each bucking hump rubbed his butt cheeks against Bram' stout, hairy legs and groin, and every brutal thrust slapped Bram's balls against his ass. The burn in his puckered hole dulled and flared, depending on the angle Bram chose.

James' lover varied his pace and angle, never giving James enough in one spot or at one time to bring him to climax, always teasing him to just before the peak, again and again, raising the physical and emotional stakes. Bram stroked over James' prostate until James howled then pulled back to torture him with slow, shallow thrusts that barely invaded his fluttering, clinging hole.

When his approaching climax threatened to make his balls explode for the third time, James squirmed and wiggled his baby smooth cheeks, tightening his ass and milking the thick shaft spearing him harder. Unable to entice Bram to finish the job with his ass, James resorted to something he knew Bram loved -- hearing James talk dirty.

"Fuck me harder, faster, caveman. Claim me. Do it now." A slight increase in Bram's rhythm encouraged him to keep talking. "That's it. Fill my ass. Make me taste it again." He grunted as the angle changed and Bram pounded over his prostate, lifting him off his feet. "Mark my heart with your cum, you bastard." James howled and pitched forward into the sheets as Bram's brutal strokes came in near machine gun speed.

"All you have to do is ask, baby. I'll fuck your sweet," Bram panted and lunged, "tight," thrust and twisted his hips, "little hole so hard, it'll remember who it belongs to even when you're too old to."

Leaning down to seal his chest to James' back, Bram released a hand from the bruising grip he had on James' hips. He reached down and tugged lightly on James' balls then wrapped his hand, slick with gel from an open jar tossed on the bed, around James' cock. At the same time, he nuzzled aside dark, sweaty curls and grabbed James' ear lobe between his teeth, biting down as his slick, tight fist roughly jerked off James' aching, engorged shaft.

"Cum for me now, baby."

Bram's rumble, so close to his ear, murmured from between biting teeth, sent a massive shiver of desire down James' arched spine. The tremors shook his entire body, forcing a deep growl of delight from the man on his back.

One full-length tug of his rod and James exploded, the sensation of orgasm heightened by the feeling of the cock buried deep inside of him pulsing and spurting at the same time, bathing his insides with what felt like scalding heat.

"Fuck-fuck-fuck-fuck me!"

Exhausted, James tried to fall flat onto the bed, but Bram was still hard and embedded deep inside of his ass. Warm, thickly corded arms wrapped around his chest and raised him up to plaster against Bram's slick, sweaty chest.

"Hmm. That's my baby." Bram licked a path down the back of James' neck, making the man shiver repeatedly. Bram purred into James' hair and licked some more. "Just relax, now. I'm not done with you yet."

"What?" The brilliant haze of receding orgasm made James languid and pliant.

"I'm not done with your sweet ass yet, baby. Not by a long shot."

Forcing James' legs apart wider, Bram moved closer between them and knelt up onto the bed, carrying James on his rigid cock. He moved slowly, supportive hands plucking at hardened nipples as he gripped James' lean body tightly to him.

Climax barely faded, James moaned with each fluid movement, Bram's hard shaft tapping his sensitized prostate in an irregular rhythm that teased and taunted, reviving his libido. James clung to Bram's arms, powerless to do more than hang on for the ride.

Grunting in time with James' asshole's fluttering rhythm, Bram advanced until he could perch comfortably on the bed. He sat back on his heels and pulled James onto his lap, snuggling James tightly against his crotch, his cock penetrating to its thick root.

Settling down onto Bram's thighs, James groaned at the change in angle and depth, amazed at the flood of sensations the position sent racing through his body. He dropped his head forward to rest his chin on his chest only to have it pulled back by a large hand in his hair. His head was brought to rest against Bram's shoulder then the hand shifted around to his jaw.

Bram's callused fingers caressed his neck then slid up to firmly grasp his chin. James' face was forced to turn, his neck arching, held in place by a vise-like grip. He mouth was instantly devoured in a ravenous kiss that stole his breath and bruised his lips. A hand played with his nipples, alternating from one to the other, pinching and tugging until they were stiff and burning.

"After tonight, you're going to be completely mine." Bram growled into James' neck, bit the flesh directly under his lips then returned to force his tongue down James' throat.

James squirmed and grunted, impaled and helpless, shivering with the sudden return of desire and need.

Bram stroked the roof of his mouth and tickled the soft palate before sliding under James' tongue and drawing it into his own mouth. He sucked and tugged on the slippery muscle, snagging it with his teeth when James dared to try and withdraw it.

Pulling James' face farther back over his shoulder, Bram ravaged his lover's lips, biting and sucking until the flesh was plump and hot. One stout, muscle-corded arm wrapped tightly around James' hips, yanking him back and down. Bram thrust his hips, moving his rigid cock in rapid, tiny, grinding jabs that worked the nerve endings at James' opening, the angle unerringly hitting James' prostate in a staccato rhythm.

Thrashing, James groaned and whimpered, straining against the unyielding hold. Sharp bolts of pain mixed with pleasure shot out from his frenzied mind, lancing down to James' widespread crotch. His balls bounced with each stroke, slapping Bram's granite firm thighs. Burning pleasure gathered like a tightly wound ball of snapping electricity, sparking and sizzling, filling his lower abdomen with an aching, desperate need for release.

Back pressed to Bram's broad, slick chest, pinned in place by the big man's raw strength and primal dominance, James flashed back to their first coupling in the darkened alleyway. Thrills of fresh excitement coursed through him. New sensations merging with recent memory heightened his responses to the rough bit of mating. James gasped and clenched his ass against the rhythm of Bram's thrusts, increasing the burn and spurring his lover to more aggressive action.

Like a demented lion possessed by a fevered, instinctive drive to dominant and tame his mate, Bram drove into James, over and over.

The dark red flush of excitement on James' skin was vibrant against the darker shade of Bram's arm. A massive arm encircled James' hips, immobilizing him, allowing him to squirming and twist without fear of being dislodged. The heated struggle magnified James' consuming lust.

Breaking the punishing kiss, Bram traced the line of James' arched throat with his moist tongue and teeth, one meaty hand still firmly gripping James' dark curls, holding his head back. The trail of stinging marks left behind made James shiver on Bram's cock, sending new jolts of electric desire through both of them. Bram purred deep in his throat, the sound wild and predatory.

"That's it, baby, Shake for me. Tremble for me. Show me how much I turn your -- sweet -- fuckable -- ass -- on." Bram punctuated each of the last four words with a powerful thrust that made James gasp, his fists already clinging white-knuckled to Bram's restraining arm.

"Come on, baby, talk to me. Tell me your tight, little ass is mine. Tell me I'm hitting home here, baby. Tight, hot, home, sweet home. It belongs to me. You elong to me now. Don't you, baby?"

James bucked and whimpered, painfully ncreasing his grip on Bram's supportive, restraining arm.

"I'll take that as your usual 'yes'." Bram encased ames' neglected cock in the circle of his thumb and orefinger and began jerking it up and down James' rigid haft. "Cum with me, baby mine." The moment Bram's urning hot palm encased the engorged rod, Bram shoved is hips forward and stilled, embedding himself as deeply s he could. Climaxing, his guttural roar of completion vas loud enough to rattle the windows.

At the same time, James cried out, frozen in place, ody arched, head back, eyes clenched in overwhelming apture. Spooned against Bram, in perfect alignment with is brawny lover, they melted into one, a stone-like nonument depicting the peak of brutally achieved mutual liss.

James thought his orgasm would go on forever. 'he heat coursing through him felt like fire, the jolts of leasure deep in his groin were like a series of electric lots, zapping and frying his nerves, expanding the ball of ensation in the pit of his crotch until it grew too large for is body to contain. When it finally exploded, he creamed with the exquisite pain/relief that raced up and ut, traveling down his limbs to shoot out the ends of his ingers and toes and the top of his head, taking with it all is energy and strength.

Collapsing back against Bram, James lolled his ead over the broad man's shoulder, rolling it so he could ace his lover. He felt his body being turned more omfortably in Bram's arm, but could do nothing to help vith the process. James lay back and let his newfound nate remain in complete control.

Despite his heaving chest and gasping breaths, Bram captured James' mouth in a gentle, thorough kiss that was anything but chaste, as he slowly pulled his sper cock out of his lover's pliant body. James' low groan was lost in Bram's mouth.

With James supported in his arms and against his body, Bram toppled over to the bed's mattress, carrying James along. He landed on his side, unwinding his long legs, and settled James beside him.

Bram pulled up the covers and curled around James, sheltering and soothing with a petting motion down the exhausted man's side and over James' wet tousled curls.

"Go to sleep, baby. Just let go."

James' eyes fluttered open but the expression in them was dazed and distant. "But we need to talk. I have to tell you how sorry I am." Despite his efforts James' eye slid shut.

Shaking his head, Bram kissed each closed eyelid. "Later. Time will take care of everything else. It always does." He kissed James' forehead. "I love you."

Forcing his eyes half-open, James looked up and murmured, "Love you too." His eyes drifted shut again, but he added, "So much," before sleep claimed him with a much thoroughness as Bram had.

After lightly kissing James' parted lips, Bram got comfortable, pulling the covers up higher and curling around his smaller lover. With a contented sigh and a heavy arm around James, Bram joined with his mate in slumber.

***

Three hours later, they lay in bed having the talk James insisted they have.

"Are you sure you're okay about tomorrow night?" James was a little hesitant to ask. He was hoping Bram's earlier answer wasn't just made in the heat of the moment.

Bram grinned and chuckled. "Hell, yes. I'm looking forward to it. Dunn was a friend of my father's. I remember his wife, Lenore. She's was a beautiful woman, even at her age."

James' eyebrows arched and he studied Bram's handsome, faintly shadowed profile. "You're an amazing man."

Laughing, Bram turned on his side to face James and rested a massive hand low on James' hip. The grip was casual, but seductive, as fingers lightly massaged James' flesh near his outer groin. "That's what my lover says."

Surprised, James snorted in disbelief then laughed. "Got a king-sized ego to go with that king-sized dick, huh, caveman?"

"You complaining, baby?" Fingers inched lower and Bram's voice dropped an octave, turning both teasing and sultry.

"Just about the ego. Everything else is just perfect." James let one hand travel south to lightly caress the organ in question until Bram stilled the action.

James smiled and surrendered peacefully. He looked around the pale green room. "Well, this christens the guest bedroom. We've had sex in the kitchen, your bedroom, on the staircase and in here." Hand in the air, James ticked off each item on his fingers. Wiggling his eyebrows rakishly at Bram he asked, "How many rooms do we have left for you to claim me in?"

Bram thread his finger through James' air-born hand and pulled it to his chest. "Six. Two more guest rooms, living room, dining room, library and den."

"Only six?" James let a mock pout purse his lips. "I'm disappointed. This house looks bigger than that."

Rolling over on top of James, fingertips playfully caressing James' ribcage as he turned, Bram pinned his lover to the bed. "Did I mention the boat I own? And I can't forget the hunting lodge in Canada? The lodge has three rooms, four if you count the screen porch."

Squirming at the ticklish touch, James gazed up into Bram's face as it hovered over his. "Oh yeah, we're definitely counting the porch."

"I thought so." Bram propped himself up on his elbows, blanketing James with his larger frame. He softly kissed James' eyelids as they fluttered closed, raining feather-light touches from his lips over the upturned face. "And the truck. When's the last time you made out in a truck?"

"The cab or flatbed?"

"Either."

"Never." James shook his head and grinned. "Unless you count being pulled across the seat for a kiss by some demanding, muscle-bound guy the first time I met him."

Bram had a smug smile on his face and a playful twinkle lit up his eyes. "Must have been some kiss if it qualified as making out."

"Oh, trust me, it was." James slid his hands up Bram's bulging arms to his broad shoulders, leaning up to plant a ghost of a kiss on Bram's partially open mouth.

"It was the start of the rest of my life."

He kissed Bram again, flicking his tongue along

the sensitive lining of the man's lower lip. He smiled at the sudden increase in Bram's breathing.

"Best kisser I've ever met." James sucked Bram's bottom lip into his mouth and teased it for a moment, enjoying the heated look beginning to burn in Bram's eyes and the rising flush on his tanned cheeks.

"Yeah?" Bram's response was a throaty, raw growl more than a word.

James nodded and ran his fingertips lovingly over Bram's jaw, lingering at the cleft in his chin. "Yeah. He's got great lips. A gorgeous hunk, too, but he can't wear plaid and he's kind of primal and aggressive."

His moist lips brushed over Bram's, teasing them with a lick then darting away, only to return again for another taste. James murmured into Bram's panting, waiting mouth.

"Good thing I'm in love with him. A real cavemmmmmmmmm --. Umph. Mmmmm."

Bram took control of the moment, treating James to one of his most memorable kisses. When he finally released his breathless lover, James snorted with laughter and squirmed a few inches away, a mock escape attempt from Bram's Neanderthal-like advances.

"Come back here, you." Playfully yanking James back under him, Bram rested his forehead on James' brow, roughly whispering in voice heavy with affection and desire, "Or do I have to drag you?"

End

Printed in the United States
221986BV00001B/33/A